DEVIOUS HEIR

THE BRENTSON UNIVERSITY SERIES

BOOK 3

BRI BLACKWOOD

BRETAGEY PRESS

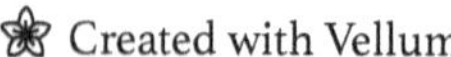 Created with Vellum

NOTE FROM THE AUTHOR

Hello!

Thank you for taking the time to read this book. Devious Game is a dark college billionaire enemies-to-lovers romance. It is not recommended for minors and contains situations that are dubious and could be triggering. The book also includes graphic violence, kidnapping, and brief mentions of a mental disorder which might also be triggering. It isn't a standalone and Nash and Raven's story is complete.

Chapter 25 might be triggering because of graphic violence.

BLURB

I wish she was here...

This was supposed to be nothing more than a game.
One where the odds were completely stacked in my favor.
But it all went awry.
Losing Raven again hurt much worse than before.
Because there was no coming back from this.
Now, I was a man bent on avenging what I'd lost.
One thing would always remain the same:
She was mine.
But there was something I didn't know:
Nothing was as it seem

PLAYIST

no tears left to cry — Ariana Grande
All I Ever Wanted — Kelly Clarkson
Anti-Hero — Taylor Swift
Million Dollar Baby — Ava Max
2 Be Loved (Am I Ready) — Lizzo
Made You Look — Meghan Trainor
Scream — Usher
Vigilante Shit — Taylor Swift
Night Changes — One Direction
As It Was — Harry Styles

The playlist can be found on Spotify.

1

NASH

OVER TWO YEARS AGO

I put another bite of lasagna in my mouth and savored the taste of it. The lasagna was homemade and absolutely delicious.

I wiped my lips with a napkin before touching Raven's hand which was resting near my glass. "I told you everything would be fine."

She looked up at me with her blue eyes and grinned. Her cheeks were slightly flushed. Usually the reason why she'd appear that way was because of me, but this time, that wasn't the case. The look of relief on her face was what I'd been hoping to see for the last couple of weeks.

It was the first time that our parents were meeting one another outside of seeing each other in passing. Raven and her mother, Clarissa, had decided to host my family at their home for dinner. Ever since that plan had been made, Raven had been nervous about how all of this would go. While I didn't blame her for being worried, it seemed as if it all was for naught.

So far, the evening had gone smoothly. Seeing the stress visibly leave her body had been something I'd been longing for since Raven's mother decided it might be a good idea to do something to bring our families together for an evening.

It was a good idea, but even I knew that both Raven and Clarissa would have an uphill battle to climb with at least one person in the room.

I looked over at my sister, Bianca, and noticed she was caught up in her phone. That wasn't surprising because it seemed that was all she did nowadays anyway.

My mother was chatting with Clarissa and that only left my father. His gaze drifted between me and Raven, and my mother and Clarissa, but he made no move to engage with either conversation.

"Nash?"

I turned my attention back to Raven.

"Can you come with me outside?"

I nodded and pushed my chair back. Raven tossed her napkin down on the table before rising from her chair. Her mother gave us a small wave and I didn't bother looking at anyone else in the room as we left.

I followed Raven to the front door and closed it behind us after we'd both walked out. The crisp air that greeted us was a lovely change from the warm house we'd just left. We took a couple of steps to the left, not standing directly in front of the door, but still had the ability to look inside the house because of the glass insert in the door.

"Everything okay?" I asked before she had a chance to speak.

She turned around to face me and immediately fell into my arms. Her words were mumbled against my chest.

I rubbed a hand down her back and said, "Little Bird, I'm going to need you to speak up because I can't hear you."

She clenched my shirt beneath her grasp before pulling away slightly. "I'm so glad this didn't go as horribly as I imagined it would."

"I won't say I told you so, but I will say I told you there was nothing to be nervous about." I paused before I continued. "But that doesn't invalidate your feelings in any way because I understand why you would be."

It was pretty obvious that my parents and Clarissa ran in different social circles. Although my parents had never said anything to me about it, it was really no surprise that my parents' friends were all pretty judgmental. It was easy to think that those views would be shared by my parents.

If they had said anything derogatory about Raven or her mother, I would have said something immediately. I tried to reassure Raven that everything would be okay and although I'd seen her visibly relax when I said something, the feeling didn't last long. The only thing that would permanently ease her nervousness was for us to make it through this dinner tonight.

"I don't want to leave a bad impression on your parents or on Bianca."

What she didn't realize was that she could never do that by being herself. Bianca didn't care about much else outside of who she was texting at the moment. My parents would support me in any way that made me happy as long as it wasn't harmful to someone else.

"Being with you makes me happy, and that's all that matters to them." At least that brought a small smile to her lips.

"You make me happy too. But there's always a thought in the back of my mind that their plans for you involve you with being with someone who is—"

She paused for a second and sighed.

"That they would want you to be with someone who is well connected and richer than I will ever be."

"I don't care what they think. You're who I want to be with. Try to push your worries aside and just enjoy tonight for what it is. It's a lovely meal between our families that was very successful."

She took another deep breath. "You're right."

"I could get used to hearing that."

"Hearing what?"

"That I'm right."

She lightly slapped her hand against my chest before she giggled. I grinned. I enjoyed making her happy and couldn't deny that it felt good to put a smile on her face.

"Feeling better?" I asked.

"Yes. But is that a shock? I'm with you, aren't I?"

"And I thought I was the one who had a way with words." I ran my hand down her cheek as I looked into her eyes. They were slightly darker in this light, but still as stunning as ever.

I lifted her head slightly and watched as she licked her lips slowly. It was pretty obvious that we both wanted what I knew was going to happen next. I bent my head and caught her lips with mine. I felt the last of the stress leave her body as she melted into me.

The feel of her lips on mine was something I've always craved and the need to have her never seemed to lessen as time went on. The intensity we shared had frightened Raven at first, but the longer we were together, the more she'd gotten used to it. Used to us.

When our kiss naturally broke apart, I brought her back to my chest and enjoyed the feel of her touch just above my heart. I wished that there were no clothes between us, but I would take all that I could get right now.

I tightened my hold on her before I looked up from where she was hugging me and back into the house. What I found surprised me. Clarissa and my father were standing close together and talking to one another. And the conversation looked anything but friendly.

I couldn't hear them through the closed door, so they weren't screaming, but they both looked pissed. Had something happened when Raven and I left the dinner table? But if it had, why weren't my mom and Bianca there? They would have been witnesses and I'm sure they wouldn't have just sat by and let this continue. At the very least, someone would have alerted both me and Raven.

No. This wasn't something that stemmed from tonight's dinner. Raven's mother and my father were heatedly talking about something that didn't occur tonight. But what could it be?

Raven sighed against my chest, and it brought my attention back to her. It felt good to alleviate some of the stress she was feeling. I smiled as I realized that I fell more in love with her tonight. When I looked at the doorway again, Clarissa and my father weren't standing there anymore. I made a note to myself to ask my father about it later, but for now, I thought nothing more of it. I had the one person that I wanted and needed in my arms. If there was anything she wanted or needed, I would make sure she had it and then some.

I could only hope that this would finally lead to her feeling more secure in us and our future.

2

NASH

PRESENT DAY

I'd enjoyed the memory of the time that my family and Raven's mother came together to share a meal. Although it had been a happy memory, it had been something that I tucked away in the depths of my mind after Raven had left. It sucked that I hadn't gotten the real story on what happened between Clarissa and my father.

Why it reappeared in my mind now was a complete mystery though.

As I was wondering about that, I heard someone talking near me and it brought my attention back to what was occurring right now.

Were the voices inside my head real or made up? Why couldn't I open my eyes?

I couldn't tell as I felt my body moving, but I knew I wasn't in control. There was no way I could be moving under my own power, I'd decided. But how the hell was I moving if it wasn't me that was doing it? Why was this starting to feel like an out-of-body experience?

What in the fuck is going on?

I needed to focus on the one thing that would help me to piece together what was going on around me: my eyesight. I willed myself to open my eyes, but my body refused. No matter how hard I tried, I couldn't get my body to cooperate with my brain. I felt a little woozy, but it still didn't feel quite real.

I could still hear voices talking but I couldn't pick up on what they were saying. I couldn't place the voices even though one of them sounded familiar. It did nothing but make my current predicament worse.

Why can't I open my eyes?

A fog that I couldn't seem to shake off had taken over my brain and clouded my mind. At least I now realized that my feet were being dragged across the ground, but the more I willed my body to fight against whatever was holding me up and pulling me, the more frustrated I became.

Why can't I move on my own? Have I been drugged?

I felt my body shifting again before I heard what I thought was a groan leaving my lips. Whatever was holding me stopped moving for a second before it continued on. Continuing on to where, though? I had no idea.

I felt the tips of my feet being dragged farther along the floor before it all suddenly came to a stop. Was this an opportunity for me to regain control of my limbs and fight off whatever the hell was taking me on a journey to who knows where? But no, my body still refused to do anything I wanted.

The next thing I knew, I lay on something. It took my brain a couple of seconds to connect that someone had laid me down in a bed.

"We need to call a doctor..." The person's voice trailed off and that raised even more alarms within me.

Were they talking about me needing a doctor? It still didn't answer any of my questions about who any of these people were or what the hell was going on.

The voices that I heard started to fade, becoming background noise in my mind. I wanted to listen to what they were saying, but apparently that was not meant to be. Had I imagined the entire thing?

And then everything went black.

3

RAVEN

TWO HOURS EARLIER

"We need to head out now."

Both Nash and I looked toward my doorway and saw Kingston Cross standing there. To say I was intimidated by his presence was putting it mildly. And that had nothing to do with the news he dropped at my feet within minutes of meeting me.

He is my half brother?

That couldn't be true, but the news flopped around my head as I zipped my bag. Kingston led the way out of the room and back to the front door. I took a deep breath as I crossed over the threshold with Nash right behind me.

Once I locked the front door of my house, Kingston turned to me and said, "We'll also make sure that someone is watching the house to make sure that nothing happens to your roommates."

I looked up at him and said, "Thank you."

I turned my attention to the vehicles that were along the street in front of my house. There were three black SUVs lined up in a row and I could see that at least the first one had a driver already inside of it. This seemed like overkill, but what did I know? Someone walked out of the shadows and my eyes nearly fell out of my head. Landon was now standing near one of the SUVs. He'd come here with Kingston? Why?

He glanced at me before he looked behind me and gave a slight nod to Nash. There was way more to this than I'd even expected and while I wanted answers, I got the feeling that this wasn't the time to ask my questions. Kingston opened up the back door of one vehicle and gestured for me to get in. I hesitated for a split second before I tightened my grip on my bag and stepped inside the SUV.

"Wait a minute," I paused and looked at Kingston wide eyed after he slid into the back seat with me and shut the car door behind him. "What the hell is going on? Where is Nash?"

My voice cracked over the last question. The nervousness I'd felt turned into pure panic. Without waiting for him to respond, I turned to the door on my side of the vehicle and tried to open it, but it wouldn't budge. Had the driver really turned on the childproof locks?

"I know we don't know each other, but I'm going to need you to trust me."

This whole thing was one huge red flag that only seemed to be increasing in size as time went on.

"What do you mean I need to trust you? You just stopped Nash from getting into this SUV with us. Where is he?"

I'd barely gotten my response out when the SUV took off without warning. I was forced to grab the car's roof and door handle in order to stop my body from moving. I hadn't had an opportunity to put on my seat belt yet. When I made a move to do so, Kingston grabbed my hand.

"Don't put your seat belt on. We won't be staying in this car for long anyway. Nash is fine."

"Excuse me? What the hell are you talking about? Is this a damn game?" I paused for a moment because, honestly, this felt like anything but. "Nothing you've said has been good enough. I want to talk to Nash now."

"I can't let you talk to Nash, but there's something I'm going to need you to do as soon as the car stops."

"You're asking a lot of someone you barely know. Especially someone that you are basically kidnapping. I want Nash and I want to go home."

"I don't want to make this harder than it has already been. But right now, you need to trust me."

I swallowed the lump in my throat as I glanced out the window. "It seems I don't have much of a choice now, do I?"

Kingston didn't respond and I turned my attention back to studying the scenery that I could see from inside of the SUV. There was no way that I would be able to open the door and throw myself out of this vehicle. We were traveling at a much faster speed than when Nash and I were driving to his cabin. I wouldn't survive with just minor bumps and bruises this time around. I hoped and prayed that we would come across the police.

Fighting them also seemed useless. While I hadn't seen them, I could almost guarantee these men had guns. I didn't consider myself weak but taking on these men would be a fool's errand.

I'm strong. I'm strong. I'm strong.

I said the words repeatedly in my head before I spoke out loud. "What do you want me to do when this SUV comes to a stop?"

"I'm going to need you to run out of the car and don't stop. Don't look back, don't wait for anyone. Just run."

"Wait, what?" Confusion clouded every thought in my head. For some reason, I couldn't process what he was saying.

Kingston sighed. He probably felt like a parent who had to repeat themselves over and over again. "You need to get away from this car as quickly as possible and don't stop to see what is going on."

"What is going to happen? Where am I running to?"

"You're going to run into the woods and get as far away from this car as possible. Here, let me take your backpack now and I promise to give it back to you. I don't want that slowing you down."

I grabbed the bag and hesitated. His words were just that: words. Right now, I didn't know if I'd ever see my belongings again, and this was the only thing I had. I was just supposed to hand it over to a stranger?

"I'll be right behind you, so you won't be alone."

I'd been alone for most of the last two years so his words affected me more than they probably should have, even if I didn't trust him completely.

This was absolutely ludicrous.

"This is the only option you have, so do as I say. You'll only have a few seconds to clear the area."

What the fuck was this guy on? Why did I have to clear the area? Nothing he was saying made any sense. "Once again, what's going to happen?"

Kingston looked at me quickly before looking straight again. "Let's just say that things are going to get loud and bright."

His words did nothing to stop the questions I had, but I

was too frightened to speak. Just about everything he said sounded like a riddle I couldn't crack. It felt as if I was so in the dark that I didn't know which way was up or down. My entire world seemed to be in a continuous loop of getting the shit kicked out of it. Now, all it felt like I could do was go along for the ride on this roller coaster, even though all I wanted to do was get off.

The next few minutes passed by in a blur and once the SUV started to slow down, I still didn't know what was going to happen next.

"Do you remember what I said?" Kingston asked.

I nodded but didn't say a word.

"When I tell you to, you're going to throw open your door and—"

"Don't look back. I got it."

"Good. Let go of your bag."

I couldn't help but hesitate again before I nodded. I handed the bag over to him and saw something out of the corner of my eye. I watched as the SUV that Nash was in drove around us.

Goodbye.

I said the word to myself, but it was meant for Nash. I prayed that it wasn't forever, much like I had the evening I drove away from Brentson after we graduated from high school. I didn't know where this evening would lead, but I only had one goal for the night and that was to survive.

The vehicle slowed down until it was almost at a standstill.

Kingston turned to me and said, "Ready... Go!"

The SUV came to a complete stop, and I did as I was told. I flung the door open and took off running. I didn't know where I was going but I kept running. Adrenaline pumped through my veins as my legs propelled me forward. Stopping wasn't an option.

How was Kingston supposed to find me if I was running through a heavily wooded area with no clear sense of where I was even going? It wasn't like I had his number to call him.

I cursed to myself when I realized I didn't have my phone on me either because it would have been really helpful right now. I must have thrown it into the bag before I left my apartment. There was nothing I could do about it, so I kept running.

The only sound that I could hear was my heavy breathing. Well, that was the case until I heard what sounded like a loud bang behind me. I jumped and I couldn't resist the urge to look over my shoulder to see what had happened. From where I was in the woods, I could see what looked like flames above the treetops in the direction that I'd come from. My heart leaped into my throat.

The only reason that I could come up with was that the SUV I'd been in exploded.

4

RAVEN

I knew I wasn't supposed to stop running, but I had to. I was in too much shock over the scene unfolding in front of me.

My mouth dropped open and I couldn't take my eyes off the flames. Listening to Kingston had saved my life.

But I was disobeying his wishes now. I needed to keep moving. As I spun around to start running again, I screamed.

Kingston was standing in front of me, his face somewhat lit up by the flames that were now to my back. He had a disapproving look on his face. If I wasn't literally running for my life, I would have thought more about how it reminded me of one that an older sibling might give their younger one when they did something bad.

"I thought I told you not to stop running?"

"Uh. It's a little hard to do that when there is a literal explosion happening behind you. I was about to start running again when you appeared right in front of me."

"Come on. Let's go."

He was going to give up? Just like that? There was no way I was letting this go. "What the hell was that?"

"I'll explain once we get in the car. We still have a little while to walk before we get there."

He walked away, assuming that I would follow him. I was pretty sure at this point that I didn't have much of a choice if I wanted to stay alive tonight. I was confident that if I did indeed run in the opposite direction, he would try to catch me. This all was very different from my experience with Nash, but why did this keep happening to me?

I jogged to catch up with Kingston. "Do I have any other options in this situation?"

He didn't answer me right away and the only thing I could hear was the sound of us walking through the woods. I heard him take in a deep breath before he finally responded. "You don't, and hopefully once this is all over, you'll be able to live the life that you want to have, and all of your questions will be answered. Stay close and try to keep as quiet as possible. I don't know all the things that could be wandering around in these woods."

"Okay."

I watched as he adjusted the strap of my bag on his shoulder as he continued walking. He didn't walk too fast, so it was easy for me to keep up with his pace even though his stride was longer than mine.

The journey through the woods lasted a lot longer than I thought it would, but that might have been because I was hoping and praying for this all to end with every step I took. I did as Kingston asked because I was afraid of what might be out here more than I was afraid of him at the moment, and that was saying something.

Kingston didn't say anything else while we walked, and for that I was grateful. I didn't want to spend this time coming up with small talk when I knew I wouldn't get the answers that I wanted yet. And that was of the utmost importance to me.

I knew that I was blindly following someone into the night, and he could easily murder me if he wanted to. But he could have also left me to die in that SUV if he wanted to and he hadn't done that.

When we were farther into the woods, he took out a flashlight and that helped guide the way to wherever the hell we were going.

We continued on in silence and every so often, I would look over my shoulder out of fear that someone or something was about to attack us. Even though I had grown up here, I had no idea where he was taking me. The woods were becoming less dense, which I hoped meant that we were getting closer to the car that Kingston had mentioned.

My legs and feet were starting to ache, but I refused to complain to Kingston. This was way more physical activity than I thought I would have been enduring today or hell, more than I'd really done since high school.

I exhaled with relief when I saw that I was right. We were getting closer to a road, but I wasn't sure where we were because my sprinting through the woods had thrown off my sense of direction. Even if I had stayed in Brentson for the last two years, I doubt I would have been able to tell exactly where we were.

"We're almost there," Kingston said in a hushed tone.

Those were the first words he'd spoken to me since he asked me to stay close to him. I didn't bother responding, giving myself more time for the questions I had to swirl around in my head.

We made our way to a road that led to an almost abandoned parking lot. I followed Kingston as he walked up to another SUV. I was wary about getting into this vehicle due to fear that it too might be blown up. Kingston opened the door for me, and I stared him down for a moment before stepping into the vehicle. He handed me my bag before closing the door behind me and walking around the front of the SUV and getting into the driver's seat.

"Now you may put on a seat belt."

I hesitated. "Is this vehicle safe?"

Kingston nodded. "Yes. This was all a part of the plan." He followed his own directions by putting his seat belt on, and that was when I followed suit.

Blowing up a car was all a part of his plan? Who in the hell would plan to blow up a vehicle?

I waited for him to start the SUV and put it into drive before I spoke. "Now can you tell me what the hell is going on? I need to call Nash and tell him I'm okay."

"No," Kingston said. "Right now is not the best time to call him. What you can do, however, is turn your phone off and hand it to me."

Shocked was the only way to describe my reaction to his words.

I stared at him before I spoke. "You're fucking with me. Why can't I call Nash? And don't bullshit me either, because I've been agreeing with a whole lot of your shit since you appeared on my doorstep."

"Right now, it's best that he thinks you're dead."

"That's ridiculous. I'm going to talk to him and tell him—"

"If you want what's best for you and him, listen to me. Don't call him or you're putting him in even more danger than he might already be in."

My mouth dropped open, then I snapped it back shut. It took me another moment before I was able to figure out how to speak again. "I'm going to need more than just that. Your word means nothing to me because I don't know or trust you. You could be pulling all of this out of your ass as you go along."

"You don't trust me after I saved your life? Me appearing on your doorstep wasn't a coincidence."

I gasped involuntarily. I'd had so many thoughts running through my mind that I hadn't focused on why he and his men had shown up at my door in the first place.

Kingston glanced at me out of the corner of his eye before turning his attention back to the road. "Do you think I'd just be coming to you, telling you that you're entitled to billions of dollars because you're the daughter of the late Neil Cross for no reason? How about one of the reasons why you were brought back here is because someone else figured that out?"

My mouth dropped open at the little information that Kingston had revealed. Could someone die from going into shock too many times in a short period of time? Because I was convinced that if this wasn't a thing already, I was about to make it one.

"My sperm donor is dead?"

I didn't know what type of reaction I'd expected out of Kingston, but he didn't give me much of one. All he did was nod but didn't provide any further details. There was only a slight change in his body language, including the clenching of his hand around the steering wheel. I wanted to keep him talking because there was so much that I didn't know. In order to fill the silence, I continued my line of questioning.

"Who would have been able to find that out? After all these years?" I paused. I realized I was acting under the assumption this man was my father. While I still had my doubts, I thought it was best to at least pretend that I believed everything that Kingston was saying. It might end up saving my life if he was the one who was behind any of this.

"There are a few people I suspect might know, but I don't see why they would want to harm you or anyone else."

"Who is on your list?"

"Not sure how much you would know about any of the names I would mention but you're going to meet one of them soon."

If I was nervous before, it didn't compare to what was coursing through my body now. My stomach felt as if it were in a pinball game within me, jerking from one side to the other with no end in sight. Being forced to run earlier didn't help the problem either.

While this wasn't going exactly how I thought it would, at least I was finally getting the opportunity to get the answers that I'd wanted for so many years. This was the moment that I'd been waiting for. If it meant being patient for a little while longer and following the things that Kingston was telling me to do, I could do it for now.

This didn't mean that I didn't have concerns. I still didn't know if I was walking right into a trap that might lead to me getting hurt or killed.

"Where are we going now?" I asked before I had an opportunity to dig any further into my thoughts which continue to swirl rapidly in my head.

He didn't respond right away, so I asked again. "Where are we going?"

"Manhattan."

"Why are we going to Manhattan?"

"Because that's where our family is."

Our family.

His words caused my heart to drop. When I was growing up, my mom had a few close friends who were like family, but really, it was always just the two of us—until it wasn't. After that, I was alone. So I didn't know how to feel about Kingston's words now. The idea of having a family felt odd, but at the same time, maybe it could be the new beginning that I was searching for.

5

RAVEN

There is no way this can be real.

I couldn't stop myself from repeating the words over and over again in my mind. I only prayed that I wouldn't say them out loud because I might look foolish. And for some reason, I cared about what Kingston thought of me.

Then again, if he knew parts of my story, he shouldn't be surprised by my reaction to any of this. I was grateful that if Kingston noticed the shock on my face, he didn't mention it. Because I knew I had to look like a deer caught in headlights as I took in my new surroundings.

I'd thought that Kingston might have been taking me to some sort of dungeon where he was going to chain me up to a wall and hold me for a ransom that would never be paid.

I could admit that my imagination was running wild with this one, but when you didn't know what the hell was going on, it was easy to let it do so. It gave me something to focus on in what was a traumatic time for me.

But I had to admit that the place that Kingston had taken

me to was beautiful. Stunning was a better word for it. I allowed myself to study every nook and cranny that my eyes could see as I took in this beautiful apartment. It was designed in neutral tones that anyone could take a step further and make their own. It had the latest appliances which probably cost more money than I'd ever seen. And of course, there was a beautiful view of New York City's skyline.

It wasn't the penthouse suite, but it was damn close. It also had to be one of the most expensive living spaces that I'd ever stepped foot in and that included the Henson family home.

"This is where you'll be staying for the time being."

Kingston had to be lying. "Seriously? But—"

"That car explosion wasn't just for show. None of this is."

"You still haven't explained why this is happening or what any of *this* means." I waved my hands around, gesturing about how enormous this truly was. "What was the point of causing all of this..."

My voice trailed off as I tried to find the word I wanted to use.

"Rambunctiousness?" he asked.

"Sure. We can go with that."

"The explosion was to throw whoever is after you off. If they think you're dead, then that gives us a temporary reprieve. You aren't in danger for the time being."

"So, you think I was being followed too?"

Kingston dipped his head before looking back at me. "I don't think you were. I know *you are*."

"First, wouldn't they have seen us run out of the SUV?

"Of course there's a chance, but I had a couple of my men, including the one who drove the car, stay closer to the scene of the explosion to see if they saw anything. Another car slowly drove by and didn't stop or try to call 9-1-1."

"How do you know they didn't do that?"

"Because my team had no issues cleaning up the mess. I also made sure that no emergency personnel would be in the area or respond."

If he was this confident in his evidence, then I could believe that whoever was after me thought I was dead as of now.

"How did you manage to make sure that no police would be in the area?"

"I have friends in high places who owe me or our family plenty of things."

"Are you talking about Mayor Henson?"

I was feeling braver the more our conversation continued. The shift was something I wanted, something I craved because there was no other way that I was going to get the answers I deserved.

"Speaking of Mayor Henson, I still don't know why I need to avoid Nash. He knows more about what has been happening to me than anyone besides me."

"Does he now?" Kingston raised an eyebrow. It was as if I'd challenged him, and he was ready to prove me wrong.

I crossed my arms over my chest. "Then, please enlighten me."

"I know who brought you back to Brentson."

I threw my hands up in the air. "Then you do know more than *I* know about what is happening to me."

This time, Kingston smirked at me like it was obvious that he was several steps ahead of me when it came to knowing what was going on. How much more about this situation was he aware of than me?

"First, let's start with why I showed up to your house today when I've known about you and how we were related for weeks."

Kingston went into a drawer in the kitchen and grabbed what looked to be a folder and a silver object that I didn't get a good look at. He walked over to me and said, "This is for you."

I froze and stared at the item in his hand. When I was finally able to drag my eyes away from his hand, I said, "What's that?"

"Information on your parents."

My lip trembled. I couldn't have predicted that I would have been given the opportunity that stood before me. I literally had information that I didn't know existed at the tip of my fingers and I couldn't move.

"You don't have to open it up around me," Kingston said. "Take your time. I can only imagine what's going through your mind. And if you want to take another DNA test to prove what you'll find in that file, we can arrange it."

I nodded, not trusting what I might say at the moment. But what did he mean by *another*?

"Now, the reason why I appeared at your house today is because we got wind of a threat against your life. We tried our best to stay out of your business, choosing to only watch you from a far on occasion, but this was too serious not to act on."

"So someone was going to try to kill me, and you heard about it. Who?"

"That we don't know. It would have made things a whole lot easier if we did."

"And this had nothing to do with the guy who tried to kidnap me? I assume you know about that."

"We do, and if Nash hadn't taken him out when he did, we would have. However, you would have been none the wiser because exposing you to that opened up a completely different can of worms."

"What do you mean?"

Kingston rubbed a hand down his face. "There's a lot you shouldn't be exposed to, especially when it comes to the Chevaliers. That's just one of them."

"And you would know because you are one." The words fell from my mouth with more confidence than I actually had.

"That's right."

It was then I heard something vibrate. Kingston's hand shot into his pocket, and he pulled his phone out then glanced at the screen.

"I have to go but make yourself at home. Hand me your phone and take this one in return."

"I don't know—"

"If I haven't earned your trust yet, I get it. But do this just in case someone is tracking your device. I should have tossed it back in the woods, but I didn't want to freak you out even more."

I grabbed the folder from him and placed it down on the coffee table before grabbing my bag. I fished out my phone and handed it to Kingston.

"Rest as much as you can, and I will be back in the morning. We can talk about anything you want to then, because I assume when you look at the folder, you're going to have a lot of questions. I may not have all the answers. This is somewhat new for me too, but I'll try to help where I can and if we need to call in some other members of our family, then so be it."

"Okay."

I dipped my head and found a hair tie on my wrist and tossed my hair into a high ponytail as Kingston walked to the door.

"If you need anything, call me, or knock on the front door. The guard standing outside will know what to do."

With that, Kingston left, and I was left alone, and I wasn't sure it was the best move.

Alone meant that I had nothing to distract myself with but my own thoughts and that was terrifying. Since my imagination had the ability to jump leaps and bounds when left unchecked, I knew that too much time to think could be a problem.

I couldn't get over how beautiful this place was and felt that I should be happy because even though my life was a shit show, for now at least, I was safe. I was grateful for every breath I managed to take because tonight could have ended so much worse.

I lifted my hand and noticed that it was shaking slightly. I took several deep breaths to compose myself before walking around the apartment.

This all felt like it was way too much. The refrigerator was fully stocked, and I found bath towels sitting on a towel warmer. It was as if everything was thoughtfully planned out for me. This hadn't come together last minute.

I swallowed hard. Kingston didn't mention what information had set this plan into motion, but it was something I needed to find out.

I walked past the bathroom once more before I gave in to temptation. That bathtub looked too phenomenal for me not to take advantage of it.

I started to run the bath and took off my sweatshirt and sneakers. The events that occurred tonight flashed in my mind.

Making love to Nash.

Kingston Cross appearing at my front door.

Separating from Nash and being rushed into a black SUV.

Watching said SUV blow up.

Walking through the woods to another car.

Pretending like I was dead.

As I was removing my T-shirt, I noticed the shakiness in my hand had become worse.

Fuck. I knew what was coming.

I didn't have panic attacks often, but I'd grown to recognize the signs. I could feel one coming on and was thankful that at least I could deal with it alone. Hopefully, taking a bath would help calm me down, because I didn't want things to get worse.

Hold on, Raven. You only have a couple more minutes until the tub fills up just the way you like it.

I squeezed the pressure point between my thumb and index finger to ease the headache that was starting to form. My hands were shaking so badly that my attempt was in vain.

Not even the panic that flew through my body could force me to freeze in place. I'd take being paralyzed by fear over my constant shaking that I assumed would only get worse. Then the stabbing pain in my stomach began.

"Take a deep breath. You're safe." I spoke out loud to no

one but myself. After repeating the newly formed mantra several times, it was enough to distract me until my bath was ready. I turned the water off and finished removing my clothes before I could think anything more of it.

I slowly dipped my body into the tub, allowing myself to be swallowed by the warm water that soon surrounded me. The panic that filled my body didn't subside, but it didn't increase either. It made me wonder if I'd made a mistake by stepping into this hot water.

Normally, baths would help provide a Zen-like environment for me, but panic attacks also tended to make me sweat, so I wasn't sure what type of reaction I would have.

My stress about whether or not I was going to have a full-fledged panic attack was for naught because the pain in my stomach finally lessened. My body didn't feel as if it were overheating so maybe the bath was doing its job.

I leaned back in the tub and tried to ignore everything else. I tried as hard as I could, but there was one thing I couldn't avoid thinking about: Nash.

A single tear fell down my cheek and I quickly wiped it away. I remembered being in a similar position when I fled Brentson the first time around and having nothing to do but wallow in the darkness of my thoughts. I'd had an opportunity to do anything I wanted, whenever I wanted, and all I could do was cry about leaving Nash. The circumstances of the two events had changed, but the result was the same. I was sitting here crying over Nash.

I wanted to find a way to contact him, but if it put his life in danger, I couldn't. I would rather wait this out and hope that we both survived this ordeal and that he would forgive me for going along with this.

Tears fell from my eyes, and it couldn't be avoided. I used my wet hands to rub across my face, disrupting their flow to the point where I didn't know if it was water from the bath or tears on my cheeks.

My breathing quickened and became shallower. I wanted to scream out in agony and pain, but my lungs felt as if they didn't have any air in them. I wrapped my arms around myself and wished that it was Nash's arms instead.

My lips trembled as I tried to calm down, but I did nothing but fail. What I hoped would be something that would relax me, turned into anything but. Giving up, I stepped out of the tub, wrapped a towel around my body and unplugged the drain to release the water. I distracted myself by finishing up a makeshift version of my nighttime routine. I walked into the bedroom and took my hair out of its ponytail.

I curled myself up into a ball on the bed and pulled the covers over my body in an attempt to fall asleep. The events that occurred tonight made that difficult, but I knew I needed the rest.

There was so much I needed to learn but based on bits and pieces of information I'd gotten from Kingston, I was wary about how much more there still was to discover. And, if I was indeed Neil Cross's daughter, I had to get used to being one of the heirs to his tarnished throne.

6

NASH

hat in the ever-loving fuck?

The pounding in my head forced me awake, but I didn't want to open my eyes. Then again, the only way I was going to be able to calm this fucking headache was by finding something that would ease the pain.

I took a chance and forced my eyes open. It took my eyes a second to adjust but it didn't take me long to realize where I was.

The bed was easy for me to recognize. The bedside table, the art on the wall, the television hanging from the wall.

It was my apartment. But what I didn't know was how I'd gotten here.

I whipped the blanket off my body and sat up. On the nightstand sat my phone and wallet. I quickly verified that I hadn't been robbed before I stood up and walked into my bathroom.

I took some medication that I hoped would ease my head, closed my eyes again, and threw some water on my face. As I let the water drip down my face while I reached for a hand towel, I realized that I felt as if I'd gotten slammed by a boulder.

Or maybe a gun was more accurate. The mark that it left was still near my temple.

I remembered watching the vehicle that Raven was riding in blow up. My shock from watching that happen was topped off by Landon hitting me in the head with his gun.

That son of a bitch.

There was a chance that I had a concussion, but I didn't care. I needed to find Landon, and now he was the only one who could give me an answer as to why Raven was murdered.

When he told me everything I wanted to know, he was going to be dead. And anyone else who was involved in this shit was going to have to face my wrath as well.

I wouldn't stop until I killed every single person.

That was all that mattered.

I would regret for the rest of my life that we hadn't had an opportunity to completely talk out our differences. None of this would bring her back, but I needed to avenge her death. That, for me, would be the first step in accepting it.

Was I still angry with her? Yes, but I would never get the answers that I wanted now. So this was the next best option. Sure, it sounded demented, but I didn't have much of a conscience when it came to seeking justice. I didn't care how long it took, even if I was hunting down every single person involved for the rest of my life. They would all pay for what they had done.

I finished drying off my face, putting my towel back where it belonged, and pushing through the pain in my head.

From my experience with football, I understood a concussion was likely, but I'd just have to find time to deal with it later. I grabbed my phone from the nightstand and looked for Easton's number. Just as I was about to call him, my bedroom door opened.

Who the hell else was in here?

When I looked toward the door, I found Easton standing there. His eyes widened slightly. I guess he was as surprised to see me standing here as I was to see him.

"What the hell are you doing in my apartment?"

"Watching over you to make sure you don't end up dead."

I raised an eyebrow at him. "Why? What did you hear?"

"I was just told to come here and wake you up every couple of hours just in case you were concussed. The doctor who came here to check you out told me to."

Confusion that was unrelated to the pain in my head was all I felt. I was missing something here.

Easton cleared his throat. "I can see that you're confused, but I don't know what happened either."

"Maybe not, but I need answers and I need them now."

I tried to move past Easton, but he put his hand on my shoulder, stopping me midstep.

"Dude, you need to slow down."

"There are things that I need to do and slowing down isn't one of them. Who the hell called the doctor, anyway?"

"I don't know. I received a text message telling me to come here and watch you. It was from an unknown number."

Of course it was. I gently held my forehead. The unknown number could be one of two options. One, it could be the person who killed Raven, Kingston, and the other passengers in that vehicle. Then again, why would they give a fuck about my well-being? Two, it could be the person who was sending me text messages before. I hadn't received a text message from an unknown number in a while. If it was them, it seemed as if they were back to their old ways. I was glad it was at least for something good this time.

Questions about whether they were involved in all of this shit too swirled in my head.

"You don't remember the doctor coming in and checking on you?"

I was worried about admitting what I did and didn't remember. I vaguely remembered hearing voices but contributed it to something I'd been dreaming up. Fuck it, he was my best friend and should know. I was tired of secrets.

"I vaguely remember but getting knocked in the head with a gun is making things a little fuzzy."

Easton did a double take. "What the hell were you doing to get hit with a gun?"

"Doing what I thought was right to save Raven, but I failed. Have you seen Landon?"

"Landon—"

"Landon Brennan."

"Not ringing a bell."

"Fuck." I said the word so forcefully that it made my head hurt more.

"Dude, for the second time, you need to slow down."

"Don't tell me what I need to do." Anger blocked any filter that might have stopped me. I made a move to attack Easton, and it was a stupid thing to do no matter how you looked at it. He was far too quick and not injured, giving him several advantages. Instead he grabbed me and stopped me from moving.

"Get a fucking grip. You shouldn't be doing all this if you have a concussion."

I knew he was right. But the anger and the pain were still there. I took deep breaths as I tried to control my feelings, but the need to kick my own ass was going away. I trusted that what we were doing was the right thing and now Raven was dead. I should have stopped Kingston and his men from leading us out of the house and into those SUVs.

It was something that I was going to have to live with for the rest of my life. There would be no bringing her back. I paused and reflected for several seconds, and it was enough to stop me from wanting to get into a fight with Easton. He must have noticed a change in my demeanor because he loosened his grip on me.

I took a step back before walking away from him. I made my way to the living room and sat down on the couch. Relief flooded through me because I was able to rest again.

"There are some things I need to explain," I said.

"That would be an excellent start."

"But there's a phone call I have to make first."

I found Landon's number in my phone and didn't hesitate to call the number. Continuous ringing was all that I heard, and it never reached what I assumed would have been a voice mail. I hung up and tried again but got the same result.

I growled and threw my phone.

If he was going to be an asshole and not answer his phone when he knew that I would want answers, then I was going to have to hunt him down myself.

7

NASH

"You saw Raven get murdered? The SUV she was in exploded and she died inside?"

Easton's words veered between question and comment as if he wasn't quite sure that he was saying the right thing. Or hell, maybe he didn't believe me. We both knew that I had a concussion, so it wouldn't be out of the realm of possibilities if I'd managed to make all of this up in my head.

I didn't blame him. What he'd said had sounded foreign to me. I almost hoped and wished that I'd had some sort of fever dream which had led me to make this all up. But I knew what I saw.

I closed my eyes when my emotions got the best of me again. I was trying to avoid being transported back to the time period right after my high school graduation. This time, instead of unleashing anger, it felt as if I might cry. Cry for the time we'd lost when she left. And the time that would never be replaced because she was gone now. Forever.

"I don't see anything on the internet about an SUV exploding in Brentson."

"Not surprised." Whoever had done it would have wiped their tracks anyway, but I knew there would be hell to pay whether it made local news or not. You didn't kill a member of the Cross family and get away with it.

Hell, if Kingston was right, you didn't kill *two* members of the Cross family and escape with your life. Whoever did it would pay.

What I couldn't explain was Landon attacking me in the car and then disappearing. My gut told me that he was one of the keys to all of this, and I needed to find him as soon as possible.

"Do you think the school knows about Raven's death?"

Easton's question brought me out of my thoughts. He'd made a good point.

"I should probably go talk to President Caldwell."

Caldwell was the president of Brentson University and had been for several years now. He and Dad would sometimes get a group together to go golfing. It eventually led to me getting his phone number in case I "needed anything" when I started at Brentson.

Easton balked at me before his expression returned to normal. "You're just going to go up and talk to President Caldwell?"

"Yes, I have his personal cell phone number. One of the last things that Raven said to me was that she was offered a full ride to attend Brentson University. Someone in the administration has to be aware of that."

Easton stared at me for a moment and then mumbled something under his breath about me being a Henson and getting my way, but I didn't care. He was only partially right about why I had the president of our university's number anyway.

"Nash, wait a minute. Why would it be weird that she received a full ride? There are numerous ways you could—"

I opened my eyes and slowly turned to look at Easton as his voice trailed off. "She didn't apply to transfer back here. She received something that said she needed to come back to Brentson if she wanted to find out what happened to her mother, and then she received a letter that welcomed her to Brentson University and said that she didn't have to pay a dime in tuition costs."

"That's not normal."

"Tell me about it." My words had a little more bite in them than I intended. "Sorry. Under a lot of stress at the moment."

"No harm done."

I changed the subject back to the issue at hand. "But first, we need to fucking find Landon. He's the only witness that I know was there and who survived."

"And he was the one who knocked you out?"

I wanted to nod but refrained. "Correct. I assume he was also the one who brought me back here."

"We don't know if he did that."

I squinted at the clock on the wall. "Someone at the front desk must have seen something. That's our first stop."

Easton gave me a weird look. "Nash, you and I both know how asinine this sounds, right?"

"Yes, I know this sounds ridiculous."

"Good, because you know I'd do a lot for you, but I wouldn't be your best friend if I didn't tell you that your plan isn't the most sound one that I've heard in recent days."

I raised an eyebrow at Easton. "Is this your way of telling me that you want out?"

"Absolutely not. I'm here for you, even if this doesn't make much sense to me. I just wanted to make sure that this is still something you want to do."

"Yes, I want to do this."

"Then we're going to do this together."

I glanced at Easton before giving him a nod. It felt good to have someone else in my corner. Right now, the fewer people who knew about this, the better, and it seemed as if whoever had done this had the same idea since this wasn't getting any news coverage as far as we could see.

"Look, I need to start moving now. I need to get some of my questions answered."

"Shouldn't you take it easy? You did get knocked out cold."

I looked at Easton to see if he was being sarcastic or if he had any doubts about my version of events. To me, the things that I'd been describing to him sounded like something out of a movie, so it wouldn't surprise me if he doubted what I was saying. Nothing in his expression indicated that he didn't believe me.

Normally, I didn't need any reassurance from anyone. I knew what I wanted and went after it. But having him not question me even when I knew how ridiculous this all sounded helped me regain my footing. I'd lost a part of myself last night, watching the woman I love die. All I'd wanted to do was keep her safe and talk through our issues and here we both ended up. I was alive and she was dead. All of the things I could and should have done played on repeat in my brain, and that included me not leaving her alone with Kingston.

Not leaving her alone with him meant that she would be walking this earth right now. Fuck.

"Since I know that you're not going to stop until you have answers, tell me when you start feeling worse, and we will call it quits for today."

"Yeah. Sure." I could deal with that, but deep down I knew that he knew that there was no way in hell I would ever call this off. However, that thought didn't need to be voiced out loud.

"I'm going to pack a small bag and then we can go see if Oscar or any of the front door staff saw what happened last night."

I threw some things into a small bag that would hopefully help me in case I did start feeling ill. I wasn't sure if my adrenaline would help me win the war going on between my brain and the rest of my body, but I was willing to do everything I could to prevent myself from getting sick.

Easton and I left my apartment and walked down to the front desk. I saw Oscar standing at the front door and began to wonder if my luck was about to change.

When Oscar spotted me, he said, "Good morning, sir. Are you feeling better?"

Easton and I shared a look before I turned and focused all my attention back on Oscar.

"Good morning to you, too. What do you mean about me feeling better?"

Oscar stared at me for a moment, and I could see the wheels in his head turning. He was probably trying to choose his words wisely. I understood where he was coming from with that. I wouldn't want to piss off one of the residents where I worked either.

"Oh, I saw that you were in pretty rough shape last night. Looks like you had partied pretty hard. But I'm glad to see you up and about right now. Is there anything I can do for you?"

"Thanks. Yes, I'm feeling better. Looks like I did have a bit too much to drink last night." I was willing to go along with the lie if it led me to the result I wanted. "Did I come home alone?"

It felt ridiculous to ask that question. But if it gave me the answers that I needed, so be it.

"No, you didn't. Two young gentlemen helped me get you to your apartment, and then I escorted them out. About five minutes later, he came in just before a doctor arrived to check on you. I figured everything was okay when you weren't taken out of here to go to the hospital. Why? Did something happen?"

I shared another glance with Easton. "No, but I am having some trouble remembering what happened last night. Would it be possible to see any footage that you might have?"

I looked over at the camera that was pointed at the front door before turning to look at Oscar.

"Of course. It wouldn't take too much to do that."

"Thank you," I said.

Oscar gestured for us to follow him over to the front desk. He grabbed a key and then we followed him into another office across the lobby.

"You came in pretty late," Oscar said as he walked up to a computer and began to type. "So it shouldn't be too hard to find the video." He searched through what looked to be security footage from the evening before and then said, "Aha. Here it is."

Just like Oscar described, I saw myself sandwiched between Landon and another guy as the two of them helped me walk into my building. I looked out of it so it wouldn't have been too much of a stretch for Oscar to think that I had been out late partying. I watched as Oscar led them to the elevator, just like he'd said.

"I've never seen them before, so I wanted to make sure they weren't trying to harm you in any way. So I went up with all of you since I also had the key to your place. I debated calling your parents."

I was thankful that Oscar hadn't called my parents because that would have been an even bigger shit show. It also would have thrown another barrier up that might have prevented me from finding out the things that I needed to know. The video played on and soon I saw Landon and his partner leave, and within minutes Easton had arrived, soon to be followed by the doctor that Easton met.

"Okay, this is super helpful. Thank you so much for taking the time to show this to us."

"Anytime," Oscar said. "If you need anything else, please let me know."

I waited until Oscar walked Easton and me back to the front door before I spoke again. "Once again, thank you so much."

"Of course," Oscar said as he held the door open for Easton and me to walk out.

When I made sure that Oscar was out of earshot, I said, "Well, that was helpful."

"Are you being sarcastic?"

"No, actually I'm not."

"Well, then I'm further in the dark on this than you are because all that did was tell me that Landon helped you get back home."

"No, what it told me was that Landon didn't give a shit about being seen. On the one hand, I'm glad he brought me back home. On the other hand, I was put in this situation by him in the first damn place."

It was pretty obvious that he was working with Kingston Cross, at least before I saw the SUV get blown up and he knocked me out. Why not delete the footage from the security system at my apartment showing me that he was the one who brought me home?

Because he wanted me to know it was him. What I didn't know was why he wanted me to know. Finding him was crucial and the first place we needed to check was Chevalier Manor because that's where he was living on campus.

I looked over at Easton before I said, "We're headed to Chevalier Manor and on the way, we should drive by the area where the explosion happened and by Raven's house. I want to see if there is anything left at the explosion site and I want to double-check if my car is still at Raven's place."

The car was the least of my problems right now, but it would be good to know if I needed to make other arrangements when it came to that.

"Do you know where the explosion happened?"

"I have a general idea."

Easton nodded. "Got it. Okay, we can go there now."

8

RAVEN

Morning came sooner than I had anticipated. Actually, that was a lie. I had been expecting it because I'd been staring up at the ceiling for a number of hours. I'd glanced at the time on the burner phone every so often and watched as the minutes turned into hours. Before I knew it, I found myself staring up at the ceiling for way longer than I thought. Sleep did come eventually, but it wasn't without a price. I'd woken up at least once last night due to a nightmare. In my dreams, I kept reliving what could have happened if I hadn't made the choices I had made last night.

One had me watching Nash be murdered in cold blood because we both refused to enter the SUVs. I didn't see where the shot had come from, only that it ended up with Nash staring at me wide eyed as his body sank to the ground. I, too, ended up on the ground, hysterically sobbing in front of his body.

Had that been what he felt like when he saw the SUV that I was supposed to be in blow up? There was no way he could have missed it even though the vehicle he was in was a decent distance from where our SUV parked.

But now I had to brush those thoughts aside because it was time to get up. I didn't know what time Kingston would be arriving, and I wanted to be prepared for anything. Well, as much as I could be.

Once I managed to get out of bed, I immediately headed into the bathroom and took my time getting ready. Normally, I might have gone into the kitchen and grabbed a cup of coffee before pulling myself together, but risking being unprepared was not an option. I threw on a fresh pair of jeans and a T-shirt and the same sweater that I'd worn yesterday before I left the bathroom and walked into the kitchen.

I purposely ignored the folder that I'd left on the coffee table in the living room. I knew it was there and I knew I had to read what was in it. But it wouldn't be happening before I had my first cup of coffee.

It took me longer than expected to figure out the coffee machine that was in the kitchen. That was mostly because it was way fancier than anything I'd ever seen before. Before the coffee had even touched my lips, the aroma from it told me that this was more than likely going to be the best cup of coffee that I had ever had. When I finally tasted the drink, I'd proven myself right. The coffee was delicious. Nothing else would compare after drinking it.

I grabbed my mug and walked over to the front door. I wasn't surprised to find someone still standing guard outside of it. Even if I wanted to leave, the guard there would make that very difficult.

With a heavy sigh, I strolled into the living room, but I still didn't grab the folder right away. I decided to enjoy the view that this place gave me. It reminded me a bit of Nash's apartment in Brentson, however there was no way to replicate the view that one sees while looking over New York City's skyline.

I slowly drank and savored my coffee as I took in the beauty of the early morning sky. In the back of my mind, I wondered how much time I had before I would be interrupted. I pulled the burner phone out of my pocket and saw that I had no new messages. Normally that would have been a relief, but I didn't know how any of the people I cared about were doing since I'd last seen them. Not being able to contact Nash hurt more than anything, but not being able to talk to Izzy also had me troubled. Was she worried? Had word gotten out about the explosion and my 'death'?

My hand shook slightly as I placed my mug on the table. Thankfully, the panic and worry that I felt this time didn't feel as if I was on the verge of having a panic attack, but I was still concerned that I might have harmed my friends in some way.

I couldn't bear not knowing. I grabbed the burner phone that Kingston had given me and texted the only number listed in it: his.

Me: *How are my roommates doing?*

When Kingston didn't respond right away, I grew even more worried. I tried to tell myself that panicking wouldn't help anything right now and I didn't want to end up in the same place I'd been in last night.

Instead of allowing myself to continue with my troubled thoughts, I looked at the manilla folder on the table which seemed to be staring back at me. There was nothing else I could do but read whatever was in that folder. I grabbed my mug and took another sip before setting it down.

It was time.

I ignored the trembling in my hand as I grabbed the folder and closed my eyes. Whatever was in this folder, I knew it would change my life forever.

I opened the folder and pulled out the items inside. I found photos, newspaper articles, and other papers. The first thing I saw was the results of a DNA test that had recently been done. Asking Kingston how he had gotten something that had my DNA on it would probably only freak me out more.

I couldn't tell what was on the rest of the papers just by skimming them, so I set them aside for later. The quickest things to look at would be the photos, so I started there.

There was a photo of my mom, Neil Cross, and a baby that was easy to identify as me based on the baby photos I'd seen of myself. Oddly enough, or perhaps not, all things considered, I'd never seen this one.

This proved that Neil Cross had met me. He knew I existed. That he likely knew about me my entire life, and he did nothing to try to maintain a relationship with me as I grew up.

I shook my head in disgust and anger as I thought about how my life might have been different if he'd been a part of it. I'd always wondered who my father was and where he was at that exact moment. My mother had given me so many excuses over the years about where my father was and why he hadn't been around, and I'd painted a picture in my mind that he didn't know I existed. If he had, why wouldn't he call or come visit?

But I was wrong. He knew I was alive this entire time.

Sadness had often come over me when I thought about my father not being in my life. It was now replaced with anger as I set the photo down.

There were handwritten letters included in the folder, which I pulled out next. I settled on the couch and pulled my knees up to my chest. I wasn't prepared for what I was about to read, but I knew I needed to.

I jumped when I heard someone at the front door. If it wasn't Kingston at the door, a plan formed in my mind that involved throwing my coffee mug at whoever was there. Much like I'd done to Nash when we were at the cabin.

The pounding in my chest slowed somewhat when Kingston entered the room. I was still nervous that he might try to hurt or kill me.

"You looked through the folder."

I nodded. "I'm not done, but I have started reviewing the things in here. When did you find out about me?"

"Pretty recently. Within the last couple of months. Why did you come back to Brentson?"

His question knocked me for a loop. It was one that I hadn't been expecting. Then again, the last twelve hours of my life I hadn't been expecting either. "I came back to find out what happened to my mother. She died in a hit-and-run car accident, but I always got the feeling that it wasn't that clear cut. I got what I thought was confirmation of that when I received a letter telling me that in order to find out what happened to her, I needed to come back to Brentson."

Kingston nodded before looking me right in the eye. "I can answer that question for you."

My lip trembled. "You can?"

"If it's something you truly want to know, I can tell you right now."

"Tell me."

"Your mother's car accident was planned, and Dad put in the call to make it happen."

Kingston's words made me nauseous. "He killed her? Your father killed my mother."

Kingston nodded. "*Our* father did. And I'm sorry."

9

RAVEN

"How do you know he killed her?" As the question left my lips, I could feel a headache growing. I believed it was a result of all of my thoughts tossing and turning in my head at his revelation.

"He taped conversations he had with others for insurance, as he liked to call it, or blackmail if we're being honest. I listened to quite a few and can confirm it. If you do want to listen to it, you could, but I suspect you don't."

He was right. I didn't want to hear this monster plotting to murder my mother. I braced myself for what Kingston's response might be to my next question. "Do you know why he killed her?"

"It's all included in that folder." Kingston leaned forward and grabbed the folder before pulling out a piece of paper.

"That letter was what I put together as the reason. You can read it if you want."

I tried to steady my hand as I took the paper from him. The letter was long and I grew more and more upset as I read each paragraph. I bit my lip as I read one of the paragraphs over again.

Raven needs to know she is your daughter. She is very much a part of the Cross legacy, and she deserves to be a part of it if she chooses to be. The hurt and pain that you've caused her won't be fixed easily, if at all. She won't be happy that we've kept this from her for so long and she deserves to hear it from you. I'm done waiting for you to make the right decision. If you don't take this opportunity to tell her, then I will.

I read the same paragraph over for a third time, allowing the words to sink in. I held the letter to my chest and closed my eyes. The urge to curl up into a ball and cry was there, but I didn't want Kingston to see my tears. I didn't want anyone to see me cry if I could help it. The struggle over how vulnerable I could actually be right now was waged inside of me, and I didn't know which way to turn. I could feel Kingston watching me, but he didn't say anything to distract from the moment I was having.

"How did Neil die?"

"I killed him."

"You killed... your own father?"

"I did. He didn't deserve to be alive anymore."

There was no remorse to be found in either his face or his words.

Just who the hell am I dealing with?

His indifference reminded me of Nash's after he killed my would-be kidnapper. Was it something they were taught as members of the Chevaliers? The lack of empathy that Nash had for Paul made sense. He didn't know him, had no relationship with him outside of what he'd tried to do to me. But for someone to view their father this way...

Given my own lack of experience with the man because he couldn't even be bothered with trying to be a part of my life, the apparent fact that he had my mother murdered to keep me from learning the truth of our connection, and Kingston's decision to kill him, it seemed pretty clear to me that my birth father wasn't a wonderful person. All of those dreams about my father swooping in and saving me couldn't have been further from the truth. They needed to be put to rest.

It was another piece of the image of him that I'd built up in my head coming apart. The idea that my mind had dreamed up of him was completely destroyed. Not that there had been much there outside of what my imagination had thrown together.

I put my fingers to my temples in an attempt to ease the ache that was pulsating in my skull. My brain had an overload of information and emotion and I still wasn't sure how to process any of it.

The ringing of a phone cut through the silence and I couldn't have been more grateful. It gave Kingston something else to focus on besides my reactions to the news that I was being told.

"Yes?" Kingston said.

I waited patiently as he listened to the person on the other end of the line. I pulled my sleeves up and the movement must have drawn attention to me because Kingston's eyes were back on me. Well, more specifically, on the bracelet on my wrist.

"You'll be here shortly?"

Who was he talking to? And why were they coming here?

"Uh-huh," he said in response to whoever had called him. "I'll see you soon."

He looked at the phone to end the call before looking back at me. "Where did the bracelet come from?"

"It was a gift."

"From who?"

I bit back the urge to respond like a smart-ass and instead simply said, "It's from Nash."

Kingston approached me and grabbed my arm. "Why didn't you say anything about it last night?"

"Because I didn't know I had to... Hey!"

Kingston unclasped the bracelet and examined it. His fingers seemed to touch every inch of it, and I was pretty sure he would be able to describe the piece of jewelry with his eyes closed in a matter of seconds, given how focused he was on it.

When he didn't say anything while he was studying it, my frustration grew. "First of all, you could have at least asked. Second of all, I didn't give you permission to look at something that belongs to me."

"I'm making sure there isn't a tracker on this."

My heart leaped at his suggestion but quickly fell. If Nash had a tracker embedded in the bracelet, he'd have been here by now. Unless something awful had indeed happened to him.

"There's nothing here. Let me put it back on."

I held out my arm and watched as Kingston clasped the bracelet back around my wrist. I didn't know what I'd been hoping for but if this was the best sign that Nash was actually okay, I'd take it.

"I need to run downstairs."

"To bring up the person who was on the phone?"

Kingston nodded but didn't give me any more details.

I debated asking what the person's name was but knew there was a good chance that I wouldn't know who they were anyway. "Is this the person who had me come back to Brentson?"

"Yes. He won't stay long."

I didn't expect him to outright confirm that, but here we were. As if I hadn't been nervous enough about Kingston arriving here this morning, now I was worried about who I was about to meet and what else I might find out from them.

Kingston began to close the door softly and I sighed. This would only be a short reprieve before even more information was told to me. Information that I wasn't sure I wanted, even though I knew I needed to hear it. Clearly, Kingston had known more about me and my family than I did, and I didn't know what to expect when it came to whoever he was bringing up here.

The first tear fell down my cheek as the door clicked shut. It was only the start of something much bigger. I'd cried more in the last couple of days than I had in years. Even when my mom died, I tried my best to remain stoic whenever I was in public. At the time, it was the only way I could appear to be strong. I didn't want anyone to feel pity for me and that had been one of the ways I coped. I knew now that being strong had nothing to do with showing my emotions in public. For me, it had everything to do with surviving and picking myself back up when I felt that the world was coming to an end.

My instincts told me to force myself to control my emotions here, but I was about to burst into tears again. At least I'd been able to hold it all together while Kingston was in here, but it was only a matter of time before he'd return, with or without his guest. I needed to focus because I didn't want to fall apart in front of Kingston or whoever was coming up with him. I'd hoped to maintain my composure because I didn't want either of them to see me cry but I was still wrestling for control. I stood up from the couch and quickly walked to the bathroom, hoping that in case they came back upstairs quickly, I had bought myself some time to pull myself together.

I sucked in too many deep breaths to count and tried to think of something, anything, other than the fact that Neil Cross had killed my mother. Now that I knew the truth, I didn't know what to do with myself other than freak out and now definitely wasn't the time to do that.

Kingston and whoever he was bringing to the apartment would know that I'd been crying based on my appearance. My red, bloodshot eyes and blotchy cheeks would give my secret away easily.

Why the hell did I care if Kingston or his associate knew I'd been crying anyway? Why was I ashamed of it? I'd just received horrific news and I was allowed to express how I felt about it.

I needed to stop arguing with myself and just let myself... be.

I did my best to wipe the tears that had fallen away and if more appeared then that was fine. It was a good thing I hadn't worn makeup because it would have been an even bigger mess to clean up. I took in a big gulp of air before I left the bathroom.

As I was walking back into the living room, the front door

opened. Kingston strolled in and another man dressed in a suit followed behind him. The stranger spoke first.

"Raven Goodwin."

"I'm happy that you know who I am, but I'm not sure who you are."

"Apologies for not introducing myself immediately. My name is Parker Townsend and I'm the reason why you're back in Brentson."

He stuck his hand out for me to shake as if he'd just told me good morning and asked me how my day was going. There was nothing for me to do but follow suit, and after we shook hands, I wiped my hand along my pant leg. Not because I was trying to be rude but because my hands were starting to sweat.

"Parker can't stay here too long as he's a busy man, but he was, by far, the best person to give you some more answers related to the questions you had regarding your mother."

"I want to know why you ordered me back here under the guise of having information on my mother."

Parker's lips shifted slightly, and I could see him thinking intently about how to respond to what I'd just said. "I didn't expect that to be your first question."

I folded my arms across my chest. "Surprise."

Being a smart-ass wasn't going to get me what I wanted but being in front of the man who had started all of this shit was irritating me.

"I brought you back here because there was something you needed to fulfill for the Chevaliers. I assume you know who we are by now."

I stared at Parker before my gaze moved to Kingston. He slightly nodded at me as if he could tell what I was thinking.

Fuck it. There was no way I was holding back what I was thinking now. I looked at Parker and said, "You're a member of the Chevaliers?"

This time, a small smirk formed on Parker's lips. "I'm more than just a member. I'm the chairman of the Chevaliers for the New York City chapter as well as the chairman of the entire organization."

"So all roads lead back to you."

"I guess you can say that."

"Then you can say why you wanted me to be back in Brentson."

"Nash Henson."

Suddenly a lump appeared in my throat as I tried to swallow Nash's name like a pill. "What does he have to do with any of this?"

"You had something to do with him getting what he wants most in this world."

"You're going to have to go into more detail than that."

Parker chuckled under his breath. "No, I don't. You've already received more information than I would have even thought of giving someone else. I'm feeling generous given the situation you're currently in."

"Well then, what else are you allowed to tell me?"

Kingston shifted his body weight. If he was growing uncomfortable with my line of questioning, he could kiss my ass.

"I can tell you whatever I want because I know everything there is to know about you. Like you still have a small scar on your knee from when you fell off your bike when you were five years old. Or how about the fact that you tried to blackmail Van Henson for money after you discovered that he was fucking other women behind his wife's back?"

I opened my mouth several times but was forced to snap it shut when no words came out. There was no way that what he'd said had just been a lucky guess. It was way too specific. "How do you know these things?"

"It's my job to know things like that. The Chevaliers took a particular interest in you when we found out about your connection to Nash and then it didn't take too much time to dig up the rest of your backstory... including the details you didn't know about."

"Is that in relation to Neil?"

Parker took his time answering my question. "The information I had was what led Kingston to gather his own proof and that's all in the documents you see before you."

Parker gestured to the folder that was beginning to feel like a blazing hot sword that wouldn't stop cutting into me since Kingston had informed me of its existence.

"I've read through several of the documents in there. A lot of it is starting to make sense and I do want to say thank you for bringing this to my attention, even if it was for your own selfish needs."

Parker's gaze narrowed as he was piecing together what I was getting at. I looked up at Kingston to get his reaction and was surprised to see a relaxed grin cross his face. It was as if he was pleased with the way I handled the situation. Given that I'd slightly flipped things so that I was in control, I would have thought that he would have been on the side of the person who was the chairman of the organization he was a member of. Apparently not.

"I don't believe for a second that you lured me back there

just because I had something to do with Nash getting what he wants most in this world."

"You're right. It's a bit more complex than that."

When Parker didn't continue, I ran a hand down my leg again to give me something to do. "What is it with all the secrecy? Why can't you tell me exactly what is going on?"

"Because I don't want to put you in even more danger than you're already in. We aren't the only ones who know whose daughter you are."

Kingston took a step forward and I noticed the furrowing of his brow. "This is why I want to get ahead of this. The car explosion was meant to buy us time and have them think that we are both dead. But we can completely take them off guard by doing one thing."

"What's that?"

"Having you walk out with the rest of the Cross family at our gala."

I didn't know how I felt about that. "Is that a good idea? Wouldn't that put a bigger target on my back?"

"But it would also be us publicly bringing you into the fold to show that if anyone wants to come after you again, they'll have to deal with us. This is, of course, only if this is the path that you want to choose."

I didn't expect to go public with this anytime soon. But if there was no way to bury it, then this might be the best option. I was still unsure.

"When do I have to have an answer for you?"

The tension in his face shifted and I noticed that he'd become more relaxed. Had he been worried I would turn him down immediately?

Parker raised his arm and checked his watch. "I have another meeting to head to."

Parker held out his hand to shake mine again, effectively ending our conversation. After our handshake was over, he turned to walk toward the front door with Kingston following behind him. I didn't know if Kingston planned to leave with him or was just walking him to the door.

I watched as Kingston and Parker briefly spoke to each other, keeping their voices low enough that I couldn't hear. Then Parker opened the door and the guard standing outside moved to the side to let Parker leave. Kingston closed the door behind him and turned back to me.

"Think about the gala, and if you want to do the things I said, I'll walk you through everything, and there won't be anything you need to worry about."

"I will. Thanks."

"By the way, we've quietly gotten permission for you to do your schoolwork virtually. Brand-new laptop should be here any minute, along with some clothes for you to pick and choose from. If there's anything else you need—"

"I can call you or ask the dude outside of my door. I know."

Kingston gave me a small smile. "Okay. I'll leave you to do your own thing now."

He opened the door and began to walk out before turning to look at me again. "If you want to have some company, let me know. I can see if my girl is free to come over."

I wished it could have been Izzy, but I understood him taking the precautions. If I did want to have someone come over right now, it would have to be on his terms. "Sure. I'll let you know."

10

NASH

My eyes scanned the road in front of us as we drove down the familiar road that I'd been on last night. I'd taken this road over the years, but after last night, its meaning to me had changed. Gone was just the thought of this being a means to an end, a way to get from point *A* to point *B*. Now it filled me with dread the closer we got to the inevitable.

"It's over here… somewhere." I pointed through the windshield.

"Are you sure?"

"Positive," I said as we continued driving. "Slow down up here."

Easton did as I said, and the SUV moved at a snail's pace as we inched down the street. My emotions over the events of the night before grew more intense and it took me biting the inside of my cheek to stop me from showing how much last night had fucked me up.

"Park up here." I'd recognized a sign on the road that I

saw just as the SUV I'd been traveling in had pulled in front of the one Raven was in. Just before my life had changed forever.

"You got it."

Easton stopped the car and threw it into park. I opened the car door and stepped out of the vehicle.

I took a deep breath and walked down the side of the road. Every step I took felt excruciating, not because of the pain that was still in my head, but from the pain that I felt in my heart. I stuffed my hands in my pockets in order to give them something to do because I wasn't sure what I would find when I reached the explosion site.

"Hold up," Easton said as he jogged behind me. When he caught up to my pace, he said, "You need to be careful."

"I'm fine."

"We both know that you're not."

I let Easton's statement hang in the air as I focused on finding where the SUV had exploded. It was proving to be harder than I thought, and it would explain why there hadn't been any press coverage about the accident. There was literally nothing to be found here.

Until there was something.

"Look over there." I stopped suddenly and pointed to the grassy area on the side of the road.

Easton looked toward the road first and watched as a car drove past us before turning to see what I was pointing at.

There was some debris from a car, but for someone who hadn't been there when the explosion occurred, they wouldn't have been able to tell what had happened.

What in the ever-loving fuck? Who cleaned this up?

"That's definitely from a car," Easton said as we saw scraps of what might have been a tire. "Do you think anyone might have heard the explosion from their house?"

"This far out from town? I highly doubt it. But the fact that someone took the time to hire what I assume was a team to clean it up…"

"It's strange. Someone wanted whoever was in that car dead but didn't want anyone to know about it. Why?"

I wanted to know the answer to that as well. We looked around the scene of the crime for about fifteen minutes before coming to terms with the fact that it would be hard to find anything else relevant to what happened the evening before. Whoever had cleaned it up had done a pretty good job here and who knew how far that debris could have been thrown from the car when everything had gone up in flames.

It became even more pressing for me to find Landon and figure out what the hell he knew about this whole thing. At the very least, he'd gotten payback on me by knocking me in the head after the explosion had occurred. At worst, he had murdered Raven and Kingston and whoever else had been in the car with them.

"Are you ready for our next stop?"

"Yes, let's head out. There is nothing more to see here."

Easton and I walked back to his vehicle, and he made a U-turn so that we could head back to Brentson. The closer we got to Raven's home, the more my heart pounded.

The ride past Raven's house did a multitude of things. It confirmed that my car was still there, parked right there where I had left it. Raven's car was still there, which only intensified the feelings I was having.

Visions of what had occurred the previous night crashed through my mind, and I gritted my teeth. There were so many things I could have done to change what occurred last night. Fighting my way through Kingston's men would have led to my being in the car with both of them and then I'd have died with them. Hell, that was better than the pain I was feeling now.

I ran a hand through my hair and pulled on it harder than intended. It did nothing to relieve the pain in my head, but it did what it was intended to do: stop me temporarily from thinking of Raven.

"Okay, let's go. I'll have someone drive my car back to my apartment."

"You got it."

"Thanks, man."

Easton looked at me out of the corner of his eye. "Thanks for what?"

"For doing all of this. Just... being here."

Easton looked taken aback by what I said. "You're welcome. I know you would do the same for me. Just remember it when the time comes."

I chuckled and it was the first time I'd felt any type of happiness since everything had occurred. "I'll be sure to remember that."

After we talked to President Caldwell and I tracked down Landon, it was up to me to work with Izzy and plan a memorial service for Raven. I didn't even know how to go about planning it because there was no body or evidence that anything had happened. At most, people would probably think she'd left town again.

What the hell am I going to tell Izzy?

My phone rang and I jumped slightly from the sound. For a brief moment, I thought it might have been Raven. I swallowed my emotions when I found Bianca's name staring back at me.

"Hey."

I tried to keep my voice leveled so I wouldn't raise any concerns with her. I would try to make sure that as few people as possible knew about Raven's death for as long as possible, hopefully giving me the opportunity to take out those responsible quickly.

"Nash, are you alright? I've called you several times."

I hadn't noticed any calls from her, but I ignored her question, choosing to answer her with one of my own. "What's wrong?"

"Mom and Dad were worried about you. They were hoping you'd be able to come to a last-minute lunch meeting today that they are dragging me to."

"I can't today, but I'll be at the next event."

Bianca sighed on the other end of the line, and I heard Easton beside me give a dry chuckle. I guess he'd heard her.

"I was really hoping you'd be a buffer between me and our parents' friends."

"I wish I could be, but I have some things I need to take care of first. But I promise I'll go to the next event or party that Mom and Dad drag you to."

"Good, because it's going to be an event hosted by Martin Cross in New York City."

My eyes widened for a second before I caught myself. The event hadn't been canceled as a result of Kingston's death in the car explosion. That raised every hair on my body.

"The Cross Family is throwing a party?"

"That would be what it is on the surface, but you know it's more about being a networking opportunity. A chance for rich people to meet other rich people."

I chuckled because she was looping us in with the same people she was somewhat criticizing. "I'll go and Easton is coming with me."

The vehicle jerked as Easton looked over at me. I could see him out of the corner of my eye, but I didn't acknowledge him.

Bianca gasped before she lowered her voice. "I don't think that is a good idea."

"I owe him big for helping me with something and what better way to repay him than making sure he has excellent food, free booze, and an opportunity to network with the Cross family and their guests?"

"You and I both know he doesn't need to network. He has connections, pretty much like we do."

"Mom loves him."

"Mom doesn't know him."

I didn't want to continue to talk about Easton with her while he was sitting next to me. "We can talk about it later. Is everything else alright?"

"Yes, of course."

"Okay then, I have to go, but I'll talk to you later."

"Bye."

I ended the call and put my phone back into my pocket. What I hadn't told Bianca was the reason I'd spontaneously decided to invite Easton was part of a plan that was quickly forming in my head. It was obvious that something was amiss here. Why would someone be planning to throw a party if their family member had just died?

I had to take every opportunity that I was given at this gala. The first step was making sure that Easton would be there. I needed someone there to keep my family occupied while I found a member of the Cross family and found out exactly what the hell happened to Raven.

11

NASH

I was out of the car before Easton stopped it fully. The ache in my head was getting a smidge worse, but I was determined to push through. Lucky for me, Easton had parked near the side entrance of Chevalier Manor, making it easier for me to sneak in through that door instead of going through the front.

My body gave me a small warning that I might have been doing too much as I stepped out of the car. It made sense for me to be a little more cautious given the condition I was in, but I couldn't seem to give a fuck about myself. This was all about finding who had killed Raven...or if there was something else going on. However, I knew I needed to keep in mind that I wouldn't be able to kill the motherfucker who caused this pain in my heart if I was involved in another incident, vehicle related or not.

It was still somewhat early in the morning and I was sure many of the Chevaliers would still be sleeping. I didn't care if I had to wake up the entire house. If I didn't get at least a lead to where Landon was while I was here, there would be hell to pay.

"Dude, take it easy," Easton warned me. Didn't he know saying that would only enrage me further?

"Back off," I said. The adrenaline pumping through my veins was moving at an alarming rate. The only thing that would calm me down was finding Landon Brennan.

"I'm just saying that—"

I looked over my shoulder and found Easton. "I know what you're trying to do, but now isn't the time. If the person you loved was murdered, you'd do anything in your power to find who committed the crime."

I paused for a moment as I realized it was the first time I'd admitted out loud that I loved Raven. I didn't care that I'd finally admitted it to someone, but it had clearly taken Easton by surprise as well, although he said nothing else. I assumed that was both to save him from having to ask another question and for me to give an answer that neither one of us was prepared for.

Both of us remained silent as we walked through the Chevalier Manor. If someone was awake at this hour, I dared them to say something to us because the only thing they would do was increase my rage.

We made our way upstairs without running into anyone and I soon found myself standing in front of Landon's room. Was it ridiculous to grow angrier just standing outside of someone's room? Yes, but the rational part of my brain was not working right now, and I had no problem admitting that.

I knocked on the door and no one answered. That part wasn't surprising to me. However, when I turned the doorknob and added a little bit of pressure, the door opened with no problem. This made me suspicious.

I suspected that someone who worked for Kingston or valued any sense of privacy would have locked the door if they weren't in the room. So either he'd been in a rush to get out and forgot, which seemed unlikely, or this was all preplanned.

When I heard Easton move behind me, I spoke immediately. "Hold on a second."

I reached into my pocket and pulled out my phone. I turned on my phone's flashlight and looked at the light switch to see if I noticed anything strange.

"What are you doing?"

"Looking to make sure that there isn't anything on the light switch."

"Why would there be?"

"I put nothing past him after last night, and I should have been more careful when I opened the door." I had a slight regret about that now, but at least nothing had happened.

"Do you think he would have set a trap?"

Now Easton and I were on the same page. "I'm not sure, but like I said, after he slammed a gun down on my head last night, I'd put nothing past him."

I flicked the switch on the wall, providing some much-needed light into the bedroom. The space was the most immaculate dorm room I'd ever seen. The bed was made perfectly. I wondered if Landon had come back here, or if this bed hadn't been slept in the night before.

There were no clothes on the floor or hanging off any furniture. No papers were strewn around. It almost looked as if this room was staged and that no one actually lived in there. I hated that we couldn't actually ruin the space because that would have given me a chance to let out some of my pent-up aggression.

"Are you sure this is Landon's room? Or is this a room that they show to prospective students?"

Easton's question made it obvious that he was having the same thoughts as me. There was being neat and clean and then there was this.

"This is his room. I'm positive," I replied. "We should look through as much as we can. I'll check his desk."

"I'll check to see if I can find a book bag or something. He might have it with him, but if it's here, I'll find it."

"Good plan." There wasn't much ground to cover here because the bedrooms here weren't that big.

Much like the rest of the room, there wasn't much on his desk outside of a few sheets of paper and a textbook. I skimmed the papers, and they contained nothing of interest to me.

I flipped the pages of the math textbook to see if anything would fall out. As I was flipping, I stopped on page 103 and found a Post-it note stuck to the page. I picked it up, and while his handwriting wasn't the best, I could read the words written on the small piece of paper:

Cross Industries Gala

Why would he need to write that down on a Post-it note? Was he planning on attending? He must have had a death wish if he thought that he would be getting in if he had been involved in the killing of Kingston Cross.

"That's strange," I mumbled.

"What is?"

"Landon had something about the Cross Industries Gala written on a Post-it note in the textbook over here."

"Do you think he is planning on going?"

"I'm not sure but given that he was at least somewhat involved in the car explosion, I wonder if he is trying to cause a bigger ruckus at the event. To make matters worse for me, this might be the only opportunity I might have to find him anytime soon."

Easton stopped moving and looked at me over his shoulder. "So you think he might have left this for us?"

I nodded. "This all has to be a setup. It's too convenient that he just happened to have written it on a piece of paper that I was easily able to find."

Landon knew I would have come for him as long as I didn't have any memory loss following his attack on me. He could have covered his tracks much better than this, including deleting the footage at my apartment.

Why was he leaving me a hint? Was this a wild-goose chase that meant absolutely nothing? I felt as if I was slowly losing my mind.

"I don't think we are going to get any more information here. It's time we head out and I'm going to call President Caldwell in the car."

"What are you doing in here?"

I turned and found Trevor standing at the door. "Looking for Landon. He was involved in an... incident and I would like to talk to him."

"He's obviously not here."

No shit. I wanted to say those words out loud, but it would get me nowhere.

"The chairman would like to see you."

I almost laughed in Trevor's face. What could Tomas possibly want to talk to me about now? I honestly didn't give a damn about much of anything at the moment, so I didn't know how well this was going to go.

But he also might have some insight into where Landon might be.

"Fine. Where is he?"

"In the meeting room." Trevor's eyes drifted between me and Easton, and I could see what he was thinking.

"He comes with me. Whatever Tomas wants to say to me, he can say it in front of him."

The walk downstairs and then down the hall was made in complete silence outside of the sounds of our footsteps. Easton was next to me, studying the art on the walls, the plaques and pictures commemorating Chevalier members who were still living and those who had died. I glanced at him and noticed the fascination on his face, as if the rich history in this building was drawing him in like a moth to a flame.

I understood the feelings going through his mind right now. It was the same feeling I had when my grandfather would tell me stories about the Chevaliers. Those warm, fuzzy feelings were now in doubt the closer I got to our meeting room. Everything about this entire situation screamed that this whole mess was a series of fucked-up events and I was in the middle of it with nowhere to escape. That was, unless I was able to sift through the bullshit and find what would essentially be the light at the end of the tunnel.

Trevor walked up to the conference room door and

knocked. When Tomas told us to come in, Easton and I followed behind Trevor, allowing him to continue to be our guide. Who knew what the hell we'd just walked in on.

"So I heard you were searching Landon's room."

"Have you seen him?" I refused to admit to what I was doing in Landon's room.

"No. Not since a couple of nights ago. That doesn't answer why you were in the room."

"I didn't realize you'd asked me a question."

Tomas's eyes narrowed, but his intimidation tactic didn't work. I was too far past caring to worry about anything that he might say if it didn't have to do with finding Landon. I didn't know how much more I could take after everything that happened.

I was teetering on the edge. I didn't know what would make me snap but the way that he was watching me looked as if he might be testing me. I was more than willing to rise up to the challenge.

"Watch yourself, Henson."

"I have nothing to be careful about."

I could sense the frustration radiating off of Tomas. He closed his eyes and shook his head once before opening them back up. Then he looked back at me.

"Why are you searching for Landon?"

"Because I need to talk to him about an incident that he was involved in."

Tomas's eyes were glued to me as he waited for me to go further but I didn't. I wasn't providing any more information than he asked for or that I felt like giving.

"What did you need to talk to Landon about that was so

serious that you needed to search his room? Did you try calling him?"

It was my turn to stare Tomas down because he made it seem as if searching Landon's room was my first choice.

"Of course I did." My words carried more bite than intended, but I didn't care. "He didn't answer his phone and I've called multiple times."

"Maybe he doesn't want to be found right now," Tomas offered.

That wasn't good enough.

"Well that sucks for him because I'm going to do everything in my power to find him. He has a lot to answer for."

"And what's so important that you need to find him right now?"

I thought about my words and decided to be truthful. I wanted to judge their reactions to my news. "Because I believe he was involved in Raven's murder."

Everyone was so quiet you could hear a pin drop.

I watched both Trevor and Tomas closely for any sign of shock or surprise, but only one of them acted as if this was news that they hadn't heard already. Trevor's eyes widened and his mouth dropped open. Whatever Tomas was feeling, he kept close to his chest. That wasn't a surprise because that was what he tended to do.

Tomas leaned back in his chair and said, "That's unfortunate."

I wasn't sure what I was expecting his reaction to be, but it sure as hell hadn't been that.

"Did you know anything about it?"

"No, I didn't. We never want to see that happen to

someone who did not deserve to die, but that's also one way for you to conquer her."

I almost charged at him, but Easton must have known I was going to do something because he placed his hand on my shoulder, stopping me. It was as if he was reminding me of all I had to lose.

"Anything related to the Chevalier leadership trials doesn't mean shit to me anymore."

Tomas studied me, probably wondering if I was telling the truth. If he didn't realize that I was willing to risk everything, then that was on him. If I didn't get the answers I needed, I didn't care what I had to do to show my anger.

I had no problem setting this world on fire and taking everything down with me.

Tomas dismissed Easton and me without interrogating me much further. It served us all much better because all he was doing was wasting my time. I still had phone calls to make and potential visits that might need to happen.

"You know I've never been here before."

Easton's voice forced me to shift my attention. I looked at him, taking in all of the Chevalier history that surrounded him. I'd made small comments about the Chevaliers to him, making sure not to tell him anything that was meant to be kept quiet to people who weren't members.

"The Chevaliers have a long history and have been hugely impactful to people and events all over the world. Mostly it's been done in secret, and while some people do know who we are, they don't know all of the things that we do."

"I'm starting to get that idea."

He seemed almost mesmerized by it all. Nothing he was

viewing was off-limits to the general public, but it was interesting to watch how what he was seeing had caught his attention and refused to let go. At any other time, I would have thought this was fascinating...

Easton shook his head and focused on me. "Dude, I don't know what happened. Are you ready to go?"

I winced. A pang in my head forced me to slow down for a moment to gather myself.

"We can go back to the apartment."

I was glad Easton said it, so I didn't have to. Admitting out loud that I was being affected by this was frustrating. I didn't have the time to sit here and nurse my injuries. But at least I could still make phone calls in the car to hopefully further along my mission.

"Yeah. Good idea." I didn't say anymore due to the potential fear that someone might have been listening in. Though the chances that anyone had woken up and had come down here to eavesdrop on us were slim. But I still didn't want to take the chance and let anything out that might be used against what I was trying to accomplish.

We left Chevalier Manor and I waited until the building was in the rearview before I pulled out my phone. I scrolled through my contacts and found the one that I wanted. Without thinking about it twice, I pressed the button that would call President Caldwell's phone.

I thought again about how I came to have the president's number in my phone and could only be grateful that my dad was the one who got him the job.

It would come as a surprise to no one that Van Henson was on the board of trustees at Brentson University. He, members of the Cross family, and several other Chevalier members who were also on the board made sure that the school's values were closely lined up with those that the Chevaliers shared. It was also why, whenever shit hit the fan, the chances of it being made public were slim. The situation with Caleb Johansen was an exception to the rule.

It was why I wasn't worried about killing Paul in the Chevalier Manor. If things had gotten out of control, it would have more than likely been swept under the rug so that I didn't have to worry about any of it. It was also why there wasn't an issue with me taking Raven to my cabin and having us both complete our schoolwork remotely without someone so much as uttering a word about it.

It paid to be in and to have friends in high places, and that included President Caldwell.

President Caldwell's phone rang and rang, increasing my irritation the longer I had to wait. I did understand that he was a busy man, but I was hoping that I'd caught him before he'd become occupied with the things he needed to do. When I'd finally gotten tired of waiting for him to answer, I hung up the phone.

"Son of a bitch," I mumbled as I moved my phone from my ear.

"He didn't answer?"

"Nope. I'm going to send him a text message to contact me as soon as he can."

I tapped my phone's screen as I thought about what I could do next. I'd run into a dead end with the search for Landon and now I had to wait for President Caldwell to get back to me about Raven getting transferred here on a full ride without her knowing anything about it.

Not to mention, the pain in my head was starting to pick up.

"There's one person I can go to about this that might be able to help, if he doesn't feel like being a complete dick."

"Who?"

"My father."

12

RAVEN

I found myself staring at the ceiling once more, waiting for sleep to take over. I was exhausted by all of the information I had learned and now I had to prepare for a big meeting with the rest of the Cross family and then a gala in a few days.

What the hell was this life of mine? Would I ever feel like I was in control of anything again?

Control had been one of the aspects that I'd focused on while I was away from Brentson. The decision to leave hadn't been my choice, but while I was gone, I had done so many things that I had never been able to while I was there. I made my own decisions while I was away without the approval of someone else.

I went to college because I wanted to. Furthering my education had always been a goal of mine, something that had been instilled within me at an early age. Even though I had always intended to go, I had been focused on Brentson University because of my relationship with Nash. Once I left,

I could have chosen to forgo college altogether, and it probably would have been the easier decision, but it was important to me, and I did it.

Just like I did everything else while I was away. I was on my own, supporting myself without anyone to fall back on, and I fucking survived. But now, I'd taken several steps back because of circumstances beyond my control. Deep down, I knew things wouldn't be like this forever. It was another challenge that I would overcome in time.

Hopefully, it would be sooner rather than later.

I rolled over onto my side and closed my eyes, begging for sleep to take hold of my body. But I couldn't turn my brain off.

Counting sheep or anything else hadn't worked. The cup of tea that I'd had before bed was lovely, but I was still awake.

Since sleep wasn't coming anytime soon, I got out of bed. A shiver ran through me, and I reached over to grab my sweatshirt to provide some warmth to my body before I walked into the other room.

I strolled into the kitchen to grab a glass of water with so many questions floating in my mind.

Did I want to do this?

You would have to be living under a rock if you didn't know who the Cross family was or how powerful they were. If they were putting together this gala, I was sure that it was going to be a huge deal and way more extravagant than the party the Hensons threw a few weeks ago.

Did I want to be pushed into whatever circus this would cause?

Was there really a choice for me in all of this?

I sighed before taking another sip of my water. The choice

to flee New York again had drifted up on my list of available options. Would it be cowardly this time given that I did have more leverage and the opportunity to put a stop to whatever was happening here?

But at what cost to the people I cared about?

Fuck.

It was no wonder that I couldn't sleep. I tucked my hair behind my ear as I put the glass to my lips again. I paused when my eyes caught sight of my brand-new laptop that had arrived today. It was resting on top of the folder filled with documents that I still hadn't taken the time to sit and read completely.

Every time I tried to convince myself to dive back into what was hidden between those pages, it opened up a gaping wound in my heart that I couldn't manage. I needed to give myself space and decided to spend the rest of the day trying to figure out how to use this laptop.

It had all the bells and whistles that one could want. Faster speeds, more storage, and better graphics were just some of the upgrades this machine had over my old computer. It made up for the ancient flip phone Kingston had given me as a burner phone.

It wasn't lost on me that the laptop also had the highest security features, including many to make sure that it would be very difficult to trace. I supposed that helped when, for the time being at least, I was supposed to be dead.

I took my glass and walked over to the couch and folded my legs underneath me as I sat down.

I couldn't help but wonder what Nash was doing right now.

Was he thinking about me as much as I was thinking about him?

I wiped away a stray tear that had drifted down my cheek without my noticing. I thought that my life had turned upside down over two years ago. But this felt different.

There were so many competing thoughts in my brain, and I couldn't make sense of it all. Maybe having a glass of wine was a better option.

Before giving in to that temptation, I pulled my laptop out and began surfing the internet in an effort to find something that would keep me occupied or make me sleepy. Or both.

When nothing caught my attention, my eyes once again drifted over to the folder on the coffee table. Ripping the Band-Aid off was the best way to do this type of thing, right?

I'd reviewed the photos, news articles, and other information, but there was one thing that was still holding me back.

After reading one of the letters that my mother sent to Neil, where she'd begged him to tell me that he was my father, I didn't think I had the courage to read the rest. I could only imagine the pain that she felt as she wrote each word, hoping to provide a better future for her child, only to have her request ignored.

And now I was about to delve into more of her private thoughts. On the one hand, this might make me feel closer to her than I was when she was alive. On the other hand, I felt as if I was about to read all about one of the most traumatic moments of her life.

With a shaky breath, I picked up the folder and began to read another one of the letters my mother sent to Neil.

The wound within me grew larger. I mourned the loss of

my mother all over again. I mourned the loss of a childhood that I could have had if my father had been more than just a worthless piece of shit.

And I cried.

13

NASH

Two mornings later, I woke up feeling refreshed. While I was still sporting a bruise on my head from the hit with the gun, my mind felt clearer. The fog that had descended on me had lifted. It had been hard for me to rest with my thoughts circling around Raven and her death. But I did end up getting more sleep than I normally would have, which was needed.

Easton stayed at his own apartment the last couple of nights, and I was glad. It was a relief not to need a babysitter anymore.

I felt comfortable enough to drive my Jaguar F-TYPE and deal with more bullshit today, so this was the perfect time to travel to my parents' home. I checked my phone before placing it in my pocket. I still hadn't heard from President Caldwell and that was a problem. I'd called his secretary yesterday, and she mentioned that he was traveling and would be returning by tomorrow, so I hoped to hear something from him by then.

The ride to my parents' home was uneventful and I took my time parking and easing myself out of my vehicle. I walked up the front stairs and opened the front door. I waited a moment to see if Charles would appear, but he didn't.

Strange.

"Nash. What are you doing here?"

I turned and found my mother walking over to me with a shocked expression on her face. It soon turned into a warm smile as she placed her hands on either side of my face.

"What happened?"

"Nothing. Everything is fine."

"Doesn't look like nothing. Did that come from football?"

Mom assumed that most of the injuries that I'd had were a result of football. Part of that was because she didn't want me playing the sport due to the dangers that could come about as a result of it. I didn't blame her.

"Yeah. There was an incident in practice and then..." I gestured to the spot on my head. "But I'm fine."

I didn't want her to know where I'd actually gotten the bruise from. It wasn't worth dragging someone else into this mess. I didn't plan on telling my father more information than was required either. The less they both knew, the fewer questions I had to answer.

"Something else is wrong."

"What?"

"I can see it in your eyes. Something else is wrong."

"The knock to my head took a lot out of me." That wasn't a lie.

"You should have called me. I could have come over and helped take care of you."

I shrugged. "I was well taken care of."

"Raven?"

I shrugged again, deciding that was the best way to answer that question. Before she could ask another, I pulled her into a hug, surprising her with more affection than we'd shown each other in a while.

It felt good to be back in her arms. All of the things that I'd been through over the last few days had taken their toll. No matter how differently we viewed things, knowing that she supported me right now was what I needed. Things could change in the blink of an eye, but right now I would relish this feeling of being loved.

I pulled away and looked down at her. "Is Dad here?"

"Yes. He's in his office. Can I get you anything before you head in there? Food? Something to drink?"

I looked back at the door and an image of me walking in there just before he told me what I now believed to be a lie about Raven entered my mind. Shaking that thought off, I looked back at my mother.

"No, I'm good. Where's Charles?"

"He has the day off today."

I could probably count on one of my hands the number of times I'd noticed that Charles hadn't been working. Of course, I'm sure there were more when I hadn't been paying attention, but watching my mother take on this role, even for me, felt strange.

My mother's voice interrupted my thoughts. "Please say goodbye on your way out."

"I will."

She patted me on the shoulder before I walked away, and

I headed toward my father's office door. I decided that the best way to make sure that this meeting didn't go off the rails, at least in the beginning, was to be courteous and knock on the door.

"Come in."

I opened the door and stepped inside. My father continued typing on his computer for a few seconds before he looked up and noticed that I was there.

"Nash. I wasn't expecting you."

"Yeah, I know. I didn't mention I was coming by."

"Well, come in and sit down."

I did as he asked because I needed to be on my best behavior. If I wanted to get any information out of him, it was better to be nice than to piss him off to the point where he would threaten to throw me out.

"How's everything going?" Small talk wasn't my forte, and I knew I shouldn't feel this awkward around my own father. But it had been something he'd fostered throughout my life with his distance and demanding, overbearing personality.

"Did you come here to tell me that you'll be attending the Cross Industries Gala?"

"I already told Bianca I'd be there. Easton is coming too."

"Fine."

I wasn't asking him if Easton could come, but if it made him feel better and less likely to argue with me on this, then so be it.

I debated with myself about whether I should bring Raven up, but the best step forward here was probably to avoid mentioning her since it would more than likely get my father riled up.

"But I didn't come here to discuss the gala."

My father crossed his arms over his chest. "Then what did you want to talk about?"

"Do you know where I can find Damien Cross?"

My father seemed taken aback by my request. "Why do you want to find Damien?"

"I have something I'd like to talk to him about."

"And are you going to share this with me?"

I'd been slightly concerned that he was going to do this, so I'd come prepared.

"It's something related to the Chevalier trials. And since he was chairman of Brentson University's chapter at one time..."

"You want to talk to him. I don't think he can help you with your next task."

"But he can give advice on what it takes to run the chapter." Thankfully, the lies were just flowing out of my mouth at this point.

"That's a good idea. You could have just texted me to get Damien's number."

"I know, but I stopped by to see Mom."

Another lie added to the ones I'd already told, and I didn't feel guilty about that at all. Van Henson got off on lying to those close to him and the general public. Nope. I didn't feel an ounce of guilt.

"Here's his number. I'll let him know that you'll be reaching out to contact him about the Chevaliers."

That wasn't so bad.

I had sat there quietly and patiently as my father found his number, relayed it to me, and then sent Damien a text.

Now, I was itching to get out of there because my mission had been accomplished. Part of me wanted to ask him if he'd heard anything about a car accident or explosion, but I didn't want him to start questioning me about why I wanted to know. He would grow suspicious and if I was being honest, he had every right to be.

But the look in my father's eyes kept me firmly in the chair I was sitting in.

"I want to go back to talking about the Cross Industries Gala."

Fuck. I thought we'd moved on from that topic.

"Sure. What about it?" My fingertips clenched the armrests of my chair. The urge to get out of there as quickly as possible to make another phone call was surging through my body, but I didn't want to draw even more attention to myself.

"You didn't mention bringing Raven along. Is everything alright there?"

Just him bringing up her name made me see red. "Like you care if it's not?"

"I was just curious since you like to bring her around to start a fight."

I couldn't help but roll my eyes. He was correct that I brought her to the party they held here in an effort to piss him off, but it went deeper than that. Much deeper. "Everything is always about you, isn't it?"

Dad scoffed. "I've heard this argument from you before."

I loosened my grip on the armrests and threw my hands up. "Because it's always the same argument! You turn everything into something against you. I wasn't here to talk about Raven."

"Tell me you didn't bring her to my gubernatorial exploratory party to make me angry."

"I didn't." It was one of the reasons I had, but it wasn't the only reason now. At the time, I honestly believed that I'd brought her as my date to show my old man up because I thought he'd slept with Raven. But now I know I also did it because I wanted to show the public that she was mine. I knew that there were whispers about it because of Brentson being a somewhat smaller town and a lot of people knowing her history and connection to this place. I wanted to show my father and everyone else that she was with me.

All I wanted or needed was to have her on my arm, walking side by side with me into that party. And through life.

I wouldn't get that chance again. What I wouldn't give to go back in time and change what had happened.

"You're such a fucking liar."

This time, I stood up. Something I should have done after I'd gotten Damien's phone number. "Or maybe this is your way of atoning for your guilt because you are the one who is the liar. Including the lie you told me about Raven."

"I've never lied about Raven."

"So, you are still saying that telling me she tried to fuck you was the truth?"

His head jerked back slightly when I said the word "fuck," as if he was disgusted that I would stoop so low as to say the word in front of him. I truly didn't care at this point because the one thing that I cared about in this world was gone.

My father glared at me. "She did try—"

"You're going to sit there and lie to my face about this? Seriously?"

"Shut up for one damn minute, Nash!"

I was pretty sure that my mother would come running in here at any second, wondering what the hell my father was screaming about. Then again, maybe she wouldn't in order to stay out of the way of his anger.

His eyes relaxed a bit before he said, "If you had given me a chance to explain, I would have told you that she tried to blackmail me when she found out that I was using a madam to find escorts. I paid her off and told her to leave town because that was the only way that I wouldn't have to tell you that she'd been looking into becoming an escort to pay for college."

I held back my anger as I processed what he'd said. Raven had been telling the truth. And it took me so long to believe her. "So you reverse blackmailed Raven and forced her to leave town."

He nodded. "I didn't expect her to come back here, but as luck would have it..." His voice trailed off.

"Were you worried that Raven would come forward and tell the truth about what happened?"

"Of course. I should have made her sign an NDA. While I still could legally go after her if she did say a word of this to the general public, my career would be tarnished anyway. There would be no coming back from it."

"Does Mom know about all of this?"

"What happens between your mother and me is none of your concern."

He had a valid point, but it wasn't good enough. "She deserves to know."

"She knows. And she's forgiven me."

"Wait, really?" Nothing he had said changed the anger I felt, but I wouldn't deny that I was shocked.

"She does. It wasn't something that we felt that we needed you kids to know about because, while we were rocky for a while, we moved forward and put the situation behind us."

My father took a deep breath and then said, "It took a lot to get to where we are now, but everything is fine. Better than fine."

"Just in time for you to run for office. How convenient."

"Your mother wants this just as much as I do."

I raised an eyebrow at his statement. Did my mother want this life? Yes. As much as he did? Now that was up for debate.

Someone chose the perfect time to text me, slightly breaking up the angry tension in the room. "Listen, I didn't come here to argue with you. I came here to get Damien's contact information and to see Mom. So I'm leaving."

My father nodded. "See you at the gala. And remember to be on your best behavior."

I didn't even bother giving a response because all it would show was that he'd gotten to me again, and I didn't want to give him that satisfaction. I turned and walked out of the room without giving him another glance. After closing his office door behind me, I walked back into the foyer.

"Mom?" I called out, hoping that she would give me a hint as to where she was.

"Yes? I'm in here."

Her voice was coming from the kitchen and before I could walk toward her, she appeared in the doorway.

"Leaving so soon?"

"Yeah. I should get back to my apartment and work on an assignment or something."

"Or something," she repeated before she chuckled. "Okay then, I won't hold you up, although I wish you would stay longer."

"I'll see you at the Cross Industries Gala."

Her face lit up. "I forgot that was coming up. Awesome. I'm glad to have both of my children in the same room as me again."

"The party you hosted here wasn't that long ago and both Bianca and I were here."

Mom shrugged. "You know how that turned out."

I did. Because I'd been the cause and I wouldn't apologize.

"See you later, Mom." I gave her a one-armed hug so as not to hit the cup of tea that was in her hand before heading to the front door. She followed behind me and watched as I unlocked my car door and climbed in.

I waved back at her as she stood at the threshold, waving with one hand and holding her cup of tea in the other.

The lovely encounter with my mother didn't outweigh the meeting that I had with my father. I was fuming as I drove home and knew that I needed to find a better way to manage my feelings because I would be in his presence again in just a few short days.

My attention was drawn from the road for a second when my phone rang. It was one of the calls I'd been waiting for.

"Hello, President Caldwell," I said once our call connected.

"Nash, I'm sorry that I'm just getting back to you. What can I do for you?"

"I had a question about another student that I hoped you'd be able to answer for me."

"Oh?"

"I want to know who paid for Raven Goodwin to attend Brentson University this year."

President Caldwell didn't respond for a moment. I could hear him suck in a deep breath and release it just before he gave me the standard answer I thought he would. "You know I'm not supposed to tell you any type of information related to Raven."

He hadn't realized that his answer actually told me more than he thought. "Just your responding in that way gives me an insight on this situation. A big power player paid to have her come back here, didn't they? There's no other reason why you would know exactly what I was referring to unless this had become a big deal."

"I can't tell you the financial status of any student attending the university."

"But that's not what you said initially. You were specific in that you couldn't tell me anything related to *her*."

His silence told me all I needed to know. I debated asking him if he'd heard about her being murdered, but I wasn't sure how much I could trust him anyway. What the hell else was he covering up and who was he covering for?

"I have to go, but if there is anything else you can offer me, please call me back."

"I will, and tell your father I said hello."

"Will do."

I hung up the phone without waiting to see if he'd reply. Was he hinting that my father knew more than he was letting on?

Once I'd arrived at my apartment, I parked my car and

walked into the lobby of my building. Anger radiated off of me. It wasn't due to my dad necessarily but having to wait for the Cross Industries Gala instead of dealing with it right now was driving me to want to commit another murder.

"Sir?"

I turned to look at Oscar as he walked up to me. I wasn't surprised by the thing that I saw in his hand.

A black envelope.

It didn't take much to know what was inside of it, but I still waited until I'd made my way up to my apartment before opening it.

Dear Nash,

The time has come for you to join us for a test of your knowledge. Come prepared but expect the unexpected.

Sincerely,

Tomas

Chairman of the Chevaliers, Brentson University

I read the letter over again twice to try and work out how I felt about it. I'd been working for the last few years to be one of the people who would be in the running for the chairmanship of the Chevaliers at Brentson University. Right now though, I couldn't care less about any tasks I needed to complete. The only thing that mattered was getting justice for Raven in the way I saw fit.

It was the first time in my life that the activities I thought I cared most about were put on the back burner. And I wasn't sure how to feel about that.

But I couldn't give up. I needed to stay focused because I was almost at the finish line.

While things hadn't worked out the way I'd hoped, I had the ability to change the course, at least for me. It was time I did so without worrying about the consequences that would be born from my actions.

14

RAVEN

I paced back and forth across the living room of this apartment as nervousness bested the rest of my emotions. It had been a long few days, and most of it was spent thinking about my mom, my sperm donor, and whether or not I wanted to be a part of what would undoubtedly be a spectacle at the Cross Industries Gala. Although I had what I thought would be my answer now, not having any reassurance from anyone or anything else in my life was bothersome.

I really thought I was making the right decision. While there were very few options I had to choose from, I couldn't count the number of times I thought I had reached a solution, only to backtrack and force myself to question whether I was right or not. I was sure being stuck here alone, other than the few times when Kingston would stop by, had done a number on my decision-making. Being secluded did give me the opportunity to reflect over and over again. For better or for worse.

There was a knock on my front door just before Kingston

strolled In. I'd been expecting his arrival and I stopped walking and watched him enter the suite.

"Everything okay?"

I nodded. "Yeah, everything is fine. I'm just lost in my thoughts."

"Reached any conclusions yet?"

I let his question roll around in my head, wondering if now I would finally have the courage to give him my answer. It was certainly harder than I'd anticipated.

I pulled on the sweatshirt I was wearing before looking up into Kingston's eyes. "I believe I have."

"Tell me."

"I will attend the gala."

"And we'll introduce you to our guests when we do introductions?"

I nodded. My nerves were still in an uproar about this all being thrown together, but there was nothing I could do about that right now.

"But first, you need to meet the rest of the Cross family. Will you be ready within the hour?"

"W—Wait, what?" My stomach dropped. I hadn't been expecting to leave the apartment today.

"Will you be ready to go in an hour?"

If I hadn't already been a nervous wreck before, I sure as hell was now. "That's not the type of thing to spring on someone."

"I wouldn't have had to if I'd known that was the decision that you would make."

"You didn't think I'd choose to go public with my connection to the Cross family?"

"Nope. And I'm not sure if I would have made the same choice."

I tucked a piece of hair behind my ear. "But I don't have the means to get out of this situation as easily as you do. We are very different people, Kingston."

"That's true. And that doesn't mean you aren't making the best choice. It's just not something I would have done."

I understood what he was saying but opening myself up this way might lead to the path of finding my happily ever after. If this led to whoever was in charge of ordering my kidnapping and wanting to harm me, either leaving me alone forever because I was a member of the Cross family or being found, then I was all for it.

I'd be able to have the life I'd been trying to rebuild since I got back here again. I would be able to stay at Brentson University and finish up my undergraduate degree. It meant that I would still be able to hang out with Izzy, Lila, and Erika. It meant that I could see Nash again.

I had no doubt in my mind that after some explaining, I could get back into the good graces of my best friend and roommates. But I knew that when it came to Nash, things were much more complicated. Although I'd done nothing wrong, I knew seeing me again after the traumatic night of the car explosion was going to be a lot. We needed to talk about so much outside of the car explosion that, in a way, it was just icing on the cake for all the fucked-up shit that our relationship had endured.

Hell, I didn't even know if we were in a relationship at the time of the incident. It had begun to feel like the start of something, but I wasn't sure what he'd been thinking on the subject. I'd thought about asking him more about how he was feeling and then all of this happened.

I heard what sounded like a device vibrating and Kingston confirmed it by pulling his phone out of his pocket. I'd swear on everything I owned that this man got more phone calls or text messages than I did in high school.

"Huh. This is interesting."

"What is?"

"It seems as if Nash has been asking around for Damien. Damien just told me that he received text messages from both Van and Nash and a phone call from the latter."

"What would he want with Damien?"

"Well, he can't very well contact me, can he?"

That was a good point. If both Kingston and I had actually died in the car accident, contacting a member of the Cross family was probably the next logical step, depending on what Nash hoped to achieve.

I paused for a minute to think. "Damien is your cousin?"

Kingston nodded. "*Our* cousin."

The expression on his face was more teasing than anything and I had to say that it had taken me by surprise. I'd only just met Kingston, but the most I'd seen of him smiling or joking around had been a small smile or two in passing. His personality seemed more stoic in nature, and it seemed that he only spoke or communicated when he absolutely needed to.

"And he'll be at this family meeting today."

"Correct."

That was good. Maybe by the time we met, he'd have some more information about Nash.

"Yeah, I have no problem going today. I can be ready pretty quickly. Is there a particular way I should dress?"

Kingston shrugged before sitting down in the armchair across from the couch.

Of course he'd chosen not to be more helpful with this subject. I left Kingston where he sat and walked into the bedroom. I made my way to the closet and eyed the clothes that Kingston had delivered to the apartment days ago for me to have a wardrobe to choose from. It didn't take long for me to throw together an outfit. A white blouse under a black blazer, black skinny jeans and black boots were what I'd settled on.

After placing my hair in a low bun, I checked the time. I was ready around the time that Kingston had wanted us to leave. When I walked into the living room, I found Kingston standing near my couch in a black hoodie instead of the black suit jacket that he'd been wearing before.

Kingston leaned over to grab something and said, "I want you to wear this. Put the hood up until we get into the SUV downstairs."

I looked at the black hoodie in his hand before looking back up at him. I was briefly confused, but I didn't argue. I put the black hoodie on, with the hood covering all of my hair and most of my face. I grabbed my purse, and Kingston led me to the door.

We said goodbye to the guard at my door and entered the elevator. I didn't say anything when Kingston pressed the button on the elevator panel that would lead us to the garage. With every floor we passed, it felt as if my stomach was sinking deeper into my body. My nerves refused to be contained, although I tried my best not to show it. We hadn't even left the building I'd been staying in yet and I already wondered if I was going to have a panic attack.

"As soon as this elevator reaches the garage, you're going to follow me, and we are going to walk right toward a black SUV. No second glances, no thinking about anything other than getting into that vehicle. Make sure the hood doesn't fall off your head. Got it?"

I nodded. "Does that mean I don't have to worry about this vehicle blowing up?"

Kingston's lip twitched. It was dark humor on my part, but I couldn't help but say it. If I couldn't try to find laughter in this situation, I might as well roll into a ball and cry for eternity. And I had to be honest, I felt like doing both during the duration of my stay in this nice apartment in the sky.

When we reached the garage, there was an SUV standing right outside the small hallway. I followed Kingston's lead and when he opened the back door of the SUV, I stepped inside.

It finally became apparent why we were operating the way we were, and I blamed the stress and my nerves for it taking me so long. This was a way to keep the fact that I was still alive a secret, and since Kingston was also supposed to have died that night, it made sense for him to be trying to remain incognito too. This almost felt like a secret ops mission and if this wasn't literally life or death, it would have been pretty cool.

The tinted windows of the SUV gave us the coverage we needed and once the vehicle pulled away from its idling place, I lowered my hood and breathed a sigh of relief. Step one was over.

"Well, that was adrenaline raising, but you could have told

me that we needed to do all of this in order to go to this meeting."

"Thought you'd figure we would be doing something like this to keep a low profile."

I looked at him out of the corner of my eye and when he didn't acknowledge me, I shook my head. This whole situation was mind blowing and there was one thing I needed to add to my list of things I was looking forward to once this was all over: seeing how my relationship with my half brother would change once all of this shit was behind us.

15

RAVEN

The ride to where we would be meeting the rest of the Cross family wasn't long, and soon, I watched as our driver pulled into another garage.

"I assume you want me to put the hood back up?"

Kingston said nothing, but he nodded. I prepared to do the same thing I'd done when I entered the SUV. I was nervous on the elevator leaving the apartment I was staying in, but the stress had turned up significantly now. I didn't know what I was getting into outside of meeting a bunch of rich strangers who had the entire world on the tips of their thumbs. The fact that they even wanted to meet was mind boggling to me.

After spending a lot of time thinking about what the gala would be like, I was surprised that Kingston and the rest of the Cross family wanted to introduce me as one of them. I knew I was the outsider here, and them being willing to let the public know I was one of them was heartwarming in a sense, but still had me wondering what was in it for them to want to include me so openly.

Someone was already standing there with the elevator waiting for us as we entered the vestibule. It provided an even smoother experience for us to reach the floor that we needed to go to. The ride up to our floor was anticlimactic and soon I found myself being swept into a conference room that was already occupied. All eyes turned to me, and I was completely intimidated.

With a deep breath, I tried not to show that my insides felt as if they were on fire as I tried to figure out how this might play out. Out of the corner of my eye, I saw Kingston taking off his hoodie and I followed suit. I had almost chosen to dress up more, but the blazer that I'd selected to wear underneath this hoodie was definitely the right move in this sea of suits. There was an older man with graying hair at his temples sitting at the head of the conference table and he looked oddly familiar. To his right was a man who clearly took after him as I could easily see the family resemblance between the two. Across from him were two other men who looked to be twins. I should have done some research before we'd come here but any attempt to be smart about this whole meeting had gone out the window.

The older man walked over to me first and held out his hand. "Hi Raven. I'm Martin Cross and welcome to Cross Industries."

"Thank you." His eyes stayed on me for longer than I anticipated, and I was starting to feel uncomfortable.

"I'm sorry. You have my brother's eyes, and it is strange being able to see them again."

That was right. Martin's name had been mentioned in one of the articles and pictures I'd reviewed in the folder that Kingston gave me. Speaking of Kingston, he'd never mentioned that I'd had Neil's eyes. I looked over at him and found him staring back at me and wondered if he'd thought the same thing when he met me for the first time.

Martin took a step back to allow the next man to walk up to me and shake my hand.

"Damien Cross. I'm Dad's oldest son. Nice to meet you."

I froze for a second before I shook his hand. I needed to find a way to talk to him about Nash. "It's nice to meet you, too."

Before I could attempt to continue the conversation with him, the other two men in the room walked over with small smiles on their faces. They seemed to be more friendly than Damien.

"I'm Broderick and this is Gage."

"You're twins," I responded, and instantly I felt silly for stating the obvious.

"That's accurate," Gage said. His smile had turned into a smirk and their energy put me slightly more at ease.

"Let's sit down and start this meeting," Martin said.

My eyes widened and Martin noticed.

"Trust me, this isn't a formal meeting, this is more of a get-to-know-you type of thing, but there is at least one matter we need to discuss."

I took a deep breath and walked over to the chair next to the one that Kingston had chosen. He was the one I knew the best out of everyone here and that provided a small sense of comfort even though I barely knew him. I folded my hands in front of me and waited for someone else to say something so that we could get this meeting started.

Martin cleared his throat and said, "Once again, welcome

to Cross Industries. We are delighted to have you here and if you have any questions about anything that I say, please ask."

I nodded, not trusting my voice.

"We have our hand in a lot of different industries all across the world. From real estate to renewable energy to investing in startups. If there's a company you can think of, Cross Industries probably has a tie to it in some capacity."

I cleared my throat because it felt as if I'd suddenly grown cobwebs in it. "I've heard of Cross Industries. I just didn't know I was... related to it."

"You're more than just related to it. This will also be a part of your legacy if you choose to go down this route."

Confusion muddled my mind. I leaned forward in my chair slightly. "What do you mean?"

"Because you are Neil's daughter, you'll have access to all that our money and reach can offer you. You are a descendant of Virgil Cross and deserve to have a piece of his legacy as much as Kingston and my sons do."

I licked my lips nervously. "You can't be serious." I looked over at Kingston before looking back at Martin. "Is this a joke?"

If all eyes weren't on me before, they were now. Martin looked at me curiously. "I wouldn't kid about something like this. You have Cross blood running through your veins and it wouldn't be right to withhold anything that was essentially a part of your birthright. They"—he gestured to his children and to Kingston—"all have had the benefits and privileges that come from having the Cross last name. I want to offer that to you as well."

Holy. Shit.

I took another deep breath and tried to keep my composure. I couldn't process what he was saying. It sounded as if he was talking in a foreign language that I'd never heard before because there was absolutely no way he was saying what I thought he was saying.

"We'll get all of the paperwork filled out so we can get you set up with your own bank accounts and make sure that whatever expenses and debts that you have are paid for. You'll be, at the very least, a multimillionaire in your own right and you'll never want for money again." Martin reached over and placed a hand over mine. "Raven, Neil didn't do right by you and nothing that I can do now will fix that. But if I can make things any easier now and for the future, it would be my honor if I could do so."

The emotions that were bubbling below the surface burst out of me like a volcano. Any hope I'd had of keeping myself composed went out of the window. I burst into tears and nothing I could do would stop them from flowing. I moved both of my hands and placed them over my mouth. I was pretty sure that was the only way that my mouth was staying closed at this point.

Kingston reached over and grabbed the tissue box and handed it to me. I thanked him through my tears and just let my emotions run wild. I felt Kingston pat me on the back. I appreciated the gesture even though I was sure that he felt awkward about comforting me. I'd come back to New York, and I'd barely had any connection to it, least of all a familial one, and now I had a half brother, an uncle, and cousins. *What is this life?*

All of the worries that my mother had about money when I was growing up had turned into worries that I'd had as I learned to navigate the world without her. And now I wouldn't have to struggle or worry about money ever again if Martin was telling the truth. It would take a lot of getting used to, that was for sure.

It took longer than it should have to calm myself down enough to form a coherent thought. I grabbed another tissue and wiped my face. At first, I tried to be mindful of the light makeup I'd put on before we left the apartment, but the tears continued to fall, making it pointless. I was regretting the makeup now.

I took several deep breaths in an attempt to compose myself even further. I tried fanning myself to dry the tears on my face and to slow my racing heart. It was awkward to have everyone still watching me as I tried so hard to not panic. At least I didn't feel a panic attack coming on, even though I wouldn't be surprised if one happened once my body came off this high.

When I finally stopped crying enough so that I could speak, I said, "I don't know what to say. Thank you? That sounds way too simple."

"Sometimes the simplest words are the most powerful. You're welcome. Shifting topics slightly, do you have everything you need for the gala?"

I shared a look with Kingston. "I have nothing actually. I didn't decide I was going until maybe a couple of hours ago."

Damien studied me for a moment before pulling out his phone. I'd probably eaten up enough of their time with my emotional outburst and tears.

"Mom can probably help out there," Broderick offered.

"Or hell, Grace could help," Gage countered.

Broderick glared at Gage across the table, and I saw

Kingston shake his head out of the corner of my eye. I couldn't fight the smile that wanted to appear on my lips.

"Broderick, Gage." The warning in Martin's voice made me think that this was a common occurrence between the two of them and I wasn't surprised. "Let's talk to our better halves and see if they want to do this. It also wouldn't hurt for you to meet them before the gala."

He was right. Plus, it would be nice to be able to talk and relate to someone who hadn't been born a Cross but came into it as an outsider.

"Shit."

Everyone's attention was drawn to Damien. He was stuffing his phone back into his pocket when my eyes landed on him.

"I need to go handle something," Damien said as he stood up from the table. "It was nice meeting you, Raven, and I'll see you at the gala."

With that, he walked out of the room. It hit me that I hadn't had an opportunity to ask him about Nash reaching out to him.

Damn it.

I didn't bother berating myself long because I really couldn't be blamed for reacting the way I did and forgetting one of the things that I'd meant to do after the fantastic news I'd received. I turned my attention to the remaining people in the room.

"This has been a very eventful day, I'm sure," Martin said as he, too, stood up. "Work is calling and we all need to get back to it. We'll work together with Kingston to make sure that you're adequately prepared for the gala. There is nothing you'll have to worry about except showing up."

"I'm looking forward to it." I smiled at Martin and stood up.

Broderick, Gage, and Kingston all followed, and we all walked toward the door. Kingston stood behind me as Broderick and Gage shook my hand and Martin paused before holding out his hand.

"I knew your mother when she worked at Cross Industries. I know she'd be happy about the woman that you've become."

Instead of bursting into tears again, this time, I held it together. I shook his hand too, and watched as he left the room.

I turned around and looked at my half brother. Before I could stop myself, I lightly punched his shoulder. The motion shocked me, but he didn't show any reaction that would have indicated that he was surprised by what I'd done. "You could have warned me that Martin was going to do that."

"I didn't know he was."

I did a double take. "Seriously? He didn't tell you any of this was going to happen."

"Nope."

"Does that upset you?"

Kingston folded his hands across his chest. "Does what upset me? The fact that my uncle is welcoming you into the family and giving you the money that you would have gotten at the same age that we all got ours?"

When he put it that way, it sounded foolish that I'd had that insecurity. I hesitated to even nod my head.

"No. I'm happy that all of this went well and that you're getting what's rightfully yours."

I grabbed my purse while Kingston grabbed the hoodies.

Once we were both in our hoodies and had them over our heads, Kingston led me out of the conference room, down the elevator, and into our waiting SUV.

"Are we headed back to the apartment?"

"Yes. I assume I'll have information about what arrangements need to be made in order to make sure that you're all set to go for the gala by the time we arrive. Be prepared because the next couple of days will more than likely be busy and intense. But you have nothing to worry about. I promise."

But there was one thing both he and Martin were wrong about. I had everything to worry about when it came to this gala because I had no idea what I was getting myself into.

16

NASH

I fixed my bow tie in the mirror one last time, taking another look at myself from head to toe. I had to admit that I cleaned up well and the bruise on my forehead had continued to fade until it was barely noticeable. I didn't want to take any chances that people might see it though, so I fixed my hair in a way that would hide the bruise before walking out of the bathroom of our hotel suite.

"Are you almost ready?" I asked Easton, who was standing in the en suite with a glass of water in one hand and his other hand resting in his pocket. We were ready a bit earlier than we originally thought we would be because we were meeting up with my family before the gala.

There was no way that Van Henson wasn't taking this as an opportunity to show off his family and he wanted us to all arrive together. It would make great optics and there would be plenty of photos taken that would be all over the internet the following day. He was determined to show himself in a good light for his campaign, and this was the perfect time to do so.

My father's assistant booked a fancy hotel suite in New York City for Easton and me so that we could avoid all of us staying with my parents at their apartment in the city. Bianca opted to stay with my parents because it made it easier for the team that my mother hired to be on hand to help both of them get ready for the evening if everyone was in the same location. We would be meeting up with them in a few minutes.

Easton pulled at his collar. When he kept adjusting it, I knew it was more of a nervous thing versus the collar making him physically uncomfortable. He cleared his throat and said, "I'm ready to go."

"Everything alright with the tux?"

"Yeah. I'm just wondering why I agreed to go to this thing. Not the biggest fan of all of this."

"You probably need to get used to it. I'm sure you'll be wearing a lot of suits and tuxedos in your future."

Easton rolled his eyes, but he knew I was telling the truth. His family was involved in shipping, among other businesses, which was how we met. Just before the beginning of freshmen year, our families had dinner with one another and the next thing I knew, we were best friends.

"This is an opportunity for you to meet more Chevaliers, if that's what you're still interested in."

"I am."

If Easton made a good impression with some of the older Chevaliers, that would be part of the battle won if he did decide that he wanted to be considered. He still would need to go through all of the rituals and tasks in order to prove himself but having some of the most powerful men in the world in your corner wasn't a bad idea.

"Okay. While we are there, I'll point out the ones that I know for a fact are members, but there might be a few that I might not know. Just remain on your game and you'll have nothing to worry about."

Easton nodded. "Got it."

We headed out of the hotel room and walked through the lobby. The doorman hailed us a cab and soon we were on our way to my parents' apartment.

Easton didn't bother talking to me, instead choosing to focus on whatever was on his phone. My thoughts wandered to what I needed to do next.

My last task for the Chevalier chairman trials was still days away, but I hadn't started working on anything related to it. I should be preparing because I needed to prove I was worthy, but I just couldn't seem to muster up the ability to care about it. Becoming chairman of the Brentson University chapter had been my goal for so long and now it was as if I'd been told that this meant nothing more than a participation trophy.

Instead, I'd been spending most of my time preparing to come face-to-face with Damien Cross. I needed to get what I wanted to say out quickly because there were going to be a ton of people at the event who would all be vying for his attention.

I ran a hand through my hair as I looked out the window and noticed that we were about a block away from my parents' building. Not only did Easton need to remain cool while in a room with a bunch of Chevaliers, but I needed to manage my emotions around my father. This was especially important if he knew more than he was letting on about Raven and the reason why she'd been lured back to town.

In no time, we were standing in front of my parents' apartment door. Before I could put my key in the lock, the door swung open, and standing there was someone I'd never seen before. To say I was taken aback by what I'd witnessed was an understatement.

The best way I could describe what was going on was organized chaos. First of all, I was shocked at the sheer number of people that were in the space. What I'd thought would just be a clothing designer and a stylist in the apartment had turned into a hair stylist, a nail technician, a makeup artist, and a couple of other people whose job duties I wasn't even sure about. That didn't even include Dad's assistant, Kali.

The amount of preparation that had gone into tonight was a clear indication of how important my parents thought this gala was.

We walked into the apartment, and I closed the door behind Easton.

"Let me take a look at these tuxes," the woman who opened the door said.

I assumed she was a part of the fashion design team.

The designer studied Easton's suit jacket before bending down to take a look at the hem of his pants. Bianca chose this time to walk into the room and I watched as she glared at Easton while he looked down at the woman at his feet before looking back up at my sister with a smirk.

She turned to look at me and said, "I see you still brought him here."

"Wonderful to see you too, Bianca."

Bianca rolled her eyes and as she was about to open her mouth, my mom walked over and interrupted.

"Can the two of you calm it down for tonight? Good evening, Easton."

Mom looked completely ready for the gala, unlike my sister, who still needed to change her clothes at the very least. Bianca spun on her heel and left the room. I assumed she was going to put on her gown.

"Hello, Mrs. Henson."

This time it was my turn to roll my eyes, because I could tell by Easton's facial expression and the way he said his greeting that he was laying it on thick for my mother. He knew how much she liked him and loved to use it to his benefit so that he could rub it in my face.

The designer sat back on her heels before standing up and moving over to examine my clothes.

I sighed. "Can we get through this night without killing each other?"

"I agree," said my father as he entered the room.

He was wearing a tux that matched mine and not a hair on his head was out of place. He looked the part of a confident politician who was ready to schmooze the night away.

The four of us made small talk and did our best not to piss each other off while we waited on Bianca. There were a few awkward pauses while we were chatting that had me mentally begging my sister to come out and put us all out of our misery. When she finally walked back into the living room in her dark-red gown, she spun around, showing the dress in motion.

My mom gasped. "You look wonderful, sweetheart."

"You do look beautiful," our father said and walked over to give her a kiss on the cheek.

I didn't take the time to wonder if he was just going

through the motions and practicing his fake compliments for tonight or if he truly meant it.

I glanced at Easton out of the corner of my eye and found him staring at Bianca. I barely controlled myself from shoving him before I whispered, "Watch it, fucker."

I don't know what had come over Easton because him watching Bianca this hard was new. He did, however, heed my warning and averted his gaze.

Kali clapped her hands together once and said, "It looks as if we are all ready to go."

I didn't realize how long I'd been waiting for someone to say those words. Everyone grabbed what they needed, and we headed off to the Olympus Hotel.

"I EXPECTED it to be fancy, but I didn't think it would be this fancy," I heard Bianca mumble beside me.

We'd just arrived at the Olympus Hotel and everything that Bianca had said, I was thinking too. It was obvious that Cross Industries knew how to throw a party because this was utter perfection. I'd known that my parents had spared no expense when throwing their most recent party at their home, but this was on a whole other level.

The finest wines and champagnes, along with appetizers, including caviar and oysters. My mother sent a look Bianca's way when she eyed a tray of drinks that a server held as he tried to do his job.

I leaned over and whispered in her ear, "We are on our best behavior tonight because who knows who is watching, remember?"

She leaned closer to me and said, "I know, but having a drink would help numb me to this bullshit."

I snorted and looked around the huge room. We were still standing near the back of the room, but up at the front, there were tables prepared for us to sit down and a stage with a podium on it. It was obvious that we were, at the very least, going to hear speeches and presentations at some point.

I looked down at the place card with my name on it before putting it in my pocket. We were at table number three so I assumed we would be sitting somewhere near the stage.

I still hadn't seen Damien yet, but I reminded myself that I needed to be patient. I just couldn't believe that they were going forward with this event after they'd lost one of their own. What were they hiding?

"You know, I'm surprised that they don't own a hotel where they could have hosted this."

"Don't give them any ideas."

It was Bianca's turn to laugh and when Easton started laughing with her, she glared at him.

I shook my head and spotted my father across the room. My father had immediately jumped into conversations with several people and had them laughing at whatever story he was telling them. He and I might not agree on much, but I did have to admit that when it came to networking and convincing people that he was the right person for just about anything, he did it with perfection.

My mom made sure to gently touch my father and he, in response, would put a hand on the small of her back, showing the people that they were conversing with that they were very in tune with one another and that they were a stable unit. Once again, this showed that you might want to vote for my father because he had the quintessential perfect family. At least, on the surface, it appeared that way.

"Nash."

I turned to face a man that was about my father's age. He looked familiar, but I couldn't place him.

"I haven't seen you since you were a little boy."

He pulled me, Easton, and Bianca into a conversation that went on longer than planned. I was happy when he finally handed me his business card and shook my hand.

"Tell your father I'll catch up with him later."

"I can do that. Hope you have a good time tonight."

"Same to you."

When he finally walked away, I glanced at the card before putting it in my pocket and turned to Easton and Bianca. "I had no idea who that was before he handed me his business card."

"Good job on faking it then," Bianca said. She glanced at Easton before moving over to stand on my other side, away from him.

Easton didn't acknowledge what she did, but instead said, "I don't see any of the Cross family members here."

I'd filled Easton in on what I'd learned since he'd stayed with me at my apartment after the explosion while we were getting ready for the gala. He knew I was on the lookout for Damien, and it was odd that they hadn't appeared to greet their guests yet.

"Yeah, I don't know what's going on there."

As if they'd heard me, someone walked up onto the stage in the front of the room and said, "I would like to have everyone take their seats. Thank you."

Most of the crowd did as requested and made their way to

their tables. When my family and Easton made it to our table, we were immediately served more drinks and water and given the option of ordering what we wanted to eat.

As I was putting my menu back down on the table, my father leaned over and said, "Elizabeth, look."

Of course, not just my mother looked when my father said to. I turned to see what he was referring to. A man who looked to be in his midthirties was walking over to the table next to us. It wasn't someone I recognized.

"Is that really him?" my mom asked and I noticed a hint of hesitation in her voice.

"It is," my father replied.

"Who is it?" I could have hugged Bianca for asking the question that was on my mind.

"It's Soren Grant." My mom's voice trailed off as if that was supposed to completely answer our question.

The name was vaguely familiar, but I couldn't place it. Was he a Chevalier? If so, he hadn't been involved, from my recollection. "Who is he?"

My father decided to answer this question. "Soren runs Grant Enterprises, mostly from his home about five minutes north of Brentson, although they have an office in New York City. He's rarely seen in public, let alone at an event like this, so there must have been a special incentive that was big enough to make him attend."

That triggered a memory. "Wait, Grant... he owns that old mansion outside of town, right?"

"That's the one."

I remembered hearing about it as a kid. We all thought the place was haunted or something because we rarely saw anyone coming in and out of the house. The stories we used to tell about that place as a result of our active imaginations had been crazy, but I wouldn't be surprised if some of them were true.

I watched as he took a seat at a table that had yet to be filled with guests. I assumed that that table, plus the one on the other side of it, would be filled with the Cross family. This was going to be interesting.

Bianca and Easton were next to me, bickering. When she'd finally grown irritated enough with what their conversation was about, she leaned over toward me. "I was hoping that you were lying about Easton coming tonight."

I studied Bianca for a second before I raised an eyebrow. "What's wrong with Easton going with us to the Cross family's gala? It gives you one more person as a buffer between you and Mom and Dad."

"It could have been anyone but him. In fact, why didn't you bring Raven?"

Like an idiot, I hadn't expected anyone to ask me about her. So I had to come up with a reason on the fly. "She was busy tonight. Wishes she could have made it."

"I haven't seen her around campus in a few days. We started running into each other at the coffee shop after we attended your football game together."

I was saved by my phone vibrating in my pocket, I took it out and read the text message.

Unknown Number: *Have a lovely time tonight. You're in for a real treat.*

Bianca glanced down at my phone. "Who was that?"

"No one," I replied.

I looked up and my eyes landed on Landon, who was standing across the room. He seemed to be scanning the periphery and the anger that I thought I had under control started to bubble to the surface.

Even after finding that Post-it note in his textbook, I didn't believe the asshole would actually have the nerve to show up here. He must be brave if he had the audacity to come here and show his face.

Before I could get up to follow him, I noticed a man in a black tux walking across the stage and up to the microphone. When he looked up, I recognized him immediately.

Martin Cross, the patriarch of the Cross family, had taken center stage.

Everyone immediately settled down and Martin gave a big, award-winning smile.

"Good evening, everyone. Let me be the first to give you an official welcome to the Cross Industries Gala!"

In response to his proclamation, he was given an enormous round of applause. When I looked back to where I'd found Landon standing before, he was gone.

Son of a bitch.

"Now I want to welcome my family out onto the stage. First, I would love to welcome the love of my life. Without her, I wouldn't be here because there is no way I would be able to do what I do without her. Selena Cross."

Martin joined the rest of the guests in giving her a round of applause. Selena stepped out onto the stage, smiling and waving at the crowd that clearly adored her. Her smile was infectious, and I found myself smiling back at her.

"Next, I would like to introduce my sons and their partners. Please welcome to the stage Damien and Anais, Broderick and Grace, and Gage and Melissa."

Each couple stepped out and waved at the crowd to more

applause. When it finally died down, we waited for Martin to continue.

"I would like to introduce to you another member of my family, and while we aren't father and son, I still view him as such. Here's my nephew, Kingston, and his partner Ellie."

What the fuck? Is this one big joke?

When I saw Kingston appear, my mouth dropped open. There's no way that I could be seeing what was in front of me.

Kingston is alive?

I felt Easton elbowing me in the gut. His reaction forced me to close my mouth before anyone else in the room saw the expression on my face. The last thing I wanted to do was explain why I felt this way.

Things started clicking into place as I held my breath. I watched as Martin turned his attention back to the microphone and to his guests in the room.

"Now, as many of you know, there are plenty of other Crosses out there, living all over the world. But we recently found out there was another Cross out there, one that we've welcomed into our family with open arms. Last but certainly not least, my niece Raven."

My brain completely short-circuited when the next person walked out, and I found crystal-blue eyes staring out into the crowd. When her eyes met mine, I saw them widen and her mouth formed an *O* shape.

She was just as surprised to see me as I was to see her.

17

RAVEN

I took a deep breath just before I knocked on the door to the penthouse suite of the Olympus Hotel. I smiled at the guard who had walked me to the door as I waited for someone to let me into the room.

The awkwardness I felt was an understatement, but after all the shit I'd been through, I knew that this was only temporary and that I could make it through tonight as well.

When I agreed to go to the Cross Industries Gala, I didn't expect that it would turn into the circus that this had become. It had been a couple of days since the meeting with my uncle and my cousins, and now it was time to get ready for the big event. I'd been invited by Selena, my aunt, to get ready in the suite with her and some of the other significant others, and I wouldn't lie and say that I wasn't intimidated as fuck. Hell, I'd only met her yesterday when she and my uncle had come by to have dinner with me and Kingston.

She'd been so sweet, and I'd immediately warmed up to her even when I didn't want to. It felt good to at least know one person in the room, but in all honesty, a big part of me hoped that no one would answer my knock so I could run away and hide back in the hotel room that had been reserved for me once I'd confirmed my attendance. Several other members of the Cross family had decided to stay on-site as well in order to make it easier for them. I decided to do so too, because members of Kingston's security team were all over the hotel and I could sleep in the next day and order room service.

When the door swung open, Selena immediately greeted me with a warm hug. I didn't realize how much I liked hugs until she pulled me in like I was one of her children. "Come on in. We are all just getting started. Would you like something to drink or eat? We ordered enough room service to feed an army."

She wasn't kidding. There was enough food to feed everyone in this room and probably all of the guests who would be attending the gala in a few hours. My stomach rumbled at the sight of all the food before me. I'd forgotten to eat something since the banana I'd had this morning because I was so nervous about tonight.

I grabbed some food that I could quickly scarf down and walked back over to where Selena was standing.

She took me over to a chair and said, "I'll let you eat and then I'll introduce you to the girls. I believe you're next for hair."

I nodded and watched as she walked away. I thought the food I'd picked out from what was essentially a buffet would be easy for me to eat quickly, but I found myself staring at all of the activity going on around me, distracting me from what I actually should be doing.

There seemed to be a flow of how everything was going.

When one person was finished in hair, they'd move on to makeup. It was too early for us to be wearing our gowns, and we wouldn't be putting those on until it was closer to the time for us to make our way downstairs.

They all seemed to know each other, and it made me further feel like an outsider. They had their stories and their inside jokes while I didn't know what they were talking about. I didn't blame them, but it did little to help the feeling that I didn't know how to relate. I jumped slightly when one of the hairstylists turned on the hair dryer and began blowing out someone's hair.

I shook my head, and as I was taking the last bite of a bagel I'd acquired, a brunette with hair slightly lighter than mine looked over at me and gave me a big grin.

As she walked over to me, she said, "Raven, right?"

"Yes, that's me."

"Hi, I'm Ellie, Kingston's girlfriend. He's told me a lot about you."

"Funny, he hasn't mentioned much about you."

"I'm not surprised. Kingston doesn't like to divulge much about his personal life and is rather quiet. Anyway, I don't think you've been introduced to everyone yet, right?"

"Selena said she was going to introduce me to everyone, but I think she got pulled away."

Both Ellie and I turned to find Selena on the phone talking to who knows who about who knows what. It was pretty obvious what had distracted her.

"I'll be happy to do it for her. I'll take your plate."

I felt weird handing her the remnants of my food, but maybe she knew where a garbage can was. Turns out, I was right, and she tossed it away before leading me over to where hair and makeup were being done. As we approached where the other women were sitting, another brunette looked up and smiled at me.

"Hi, I'm Anais. I'm Damien's fiancée."

"She's also my best friend, but apparently that's not a qualifier anymore."

Anais chuckled as she stuck out her hand. I immediately noticed the ring on her ring finger. She looked up at Ellie and said, "Keep teasing me and I'll find another maid of honor."

"You have to actually make wedding plans first for me to feel threatened."

I laughed at their banter back and forth. It reminded me of some of the conversations I'd had with Izzy.

"The blonde next to Anais is Grace, and the woman at the other end of the room on the phone with the curly brown hair is Melissa. They are dating Broderick and Gage, respectively."

Grace gave me a small wave. Melissa was too busy staring at her phone, and she wasn't paying attention to our introductions.

Ellie noticed I was watching Melissa and said, "She is probably doing work even though we all agreed to take the day off so that we would have one less thing we needed to worry about when it came to this gala. She's managing one of the empire's new acquisitions as they become a part of Cross Industries."

I was confused. "What do you mean by 'empire'?"

"I jokingly refer to Cross Industries as an 'empire' because they seem to be involved in so many businesses."

I could understand her logic. It also explained all of the money they'd seemed to acquire and continue to do so.

As if she'd known we were talking about her, Melissa put her phone in her pocket and walked back over to the group.

"I'm so sorry about that. Work never seems to leave me alone." She turned and looked at me. "You must be Raven, Kingston's half sister. I'm Melissa."

I wondered if someone had explained to the group the reason why I was barging in on their beauty session.

"Yes, I am. It's lovely to meet you."

"I'm done with hair," Anais announced and she stood up from her chair. She stretched her arms above her head before grabbing her things. "I think you're next, Raven."

I nodded as Anais moved out of the way. I took her seat and took my hair out of the ponytail I'd thrown it in. Once the hairstylist examined my hair, she asked me what I wanted, and I thought about what the best hairstyle would be to accentuate my dress and the whole look. I glanced down at the bracelet that Nash had given me before looking up at the hairstylist. "How about a sleek updo?"

"I was thinking the same thing. I'll have your hair done in no time."

I reached down to pull out my phone and realized there was nothing to keep me occupied on that phone anyway, because the only thing I could use it for was to contact Kingston. I hoped with tonight's announcement that I could get my phone back and then I'd be able to contact Nash and Izzy.

Announcing that I was a part of the Cross family was the right choice. I was doing the right thing.

"Oh, you're getting your hair done now. Good," Selena said as she entered the room. "I'm sorry that I couldn't introduce you to everyone."

"No worries. Ellie did a fine job of introducing me to everyone here."

Selena smiled at who I assumed was Ellie over my shoulder before turning back to me. "I'm glad. Well, if you need anything, please, don't hesitate to ask. I'm next for makeup."

She walked away and I chose to sit back and enjoy having my hair done. I couldn't remember the last time I'd had my hair done outside of preparing for the Henson's party where Nash decided to show me off like a trophy that he'd won. I knew it was for his father's benefit more than anything, but the intent was still the same. The moment felt tainted by what Nash intended to do and this felt different.

I was nervous about what would happen tonight, but I was determined to enjoy this pampering session. After everything that had happened, I was more than ready to not do anything outside of getting dressed for the gala.

The whole pampering process went smoothly and soon I found myself standing in a long black gown that had a deep *v* in the front and my back exposed. Wearing my hair up had been the best idea.

I put on a dainty necklace and kept the bracelet that Nash had given me on. It was amazing how it seemed to go with everything. Soon, the entire group of women was standing around, complimenting each other on how good everyone looked.

When there was a knock on the door, Selena walked over and opened it. In strolled all of the Cross men in black tuxes. To the casual observer, it would seem as if they were all dressed in the same tuxedos, but I noticed a slight difference with each suit.

Kingston gave Ellie a kiss on the cheek, I assumed to avoid messing up her makeup before he walked over to me. "You clean up well, Raven."

"I could say the same about you. Then again, I usually see you in a suit, so this isn't far off."

Kingston laughed and it changed his whole face. Ellie walked over to us and looped her arm into his. "Kingston's a lucky man tonight. He gets to have two dates."

"Wait a minute, do you mean me?"

Ellie nodded. "We're walking down to the ballroom together."

"Uncle Martin mentioned that he was going to make an announcement for each of us at the gala, so follow our lead and everything will be fine."

"So is that how he's going to say that I'm a member of the family?"

"That's right." Kingston looked at his watch and said, "We need to start heading down now."

It was showtime.

18

RAVEN

I stood backstage as I waited for my name to be announced by Martin Cross. I'd been on what felt like the edge of my seat since I'd knocked on the door of the penthouse suite and now I was waiting for my name to be broadcasted to a bunch of rich strangers in a ballroom. There would be no coming back from this.

To say I hadn't expected this would be an understatement. I'd gone into today with no expectations outside of what this might mean for protecting myself and those I cared about. Instead, I was shown so much more. Maybe it was my own preconceived emotions that played a role, but I hadn't been expecting everyone to be as kind and welcoming as they were. Everyone seemed loyal to one another, and you could see how tight a group the Cross family was. This whole day had been a whirlwind and I was just along for the ride at this point.

I twiddled my thumbs as Martin announced his sons and their partners and the three couples left me with Kingston and Ellie. Ellie turned around and looked at me. "Are you okay?"

"I am. Thanks for asking," I replied.

"It will all be over shortly," Kingston said.

We turned as we heard Martin announce Kingston and Ellie by name and together, they walked out, leaving me all alone as the last one behind this curtain. My heart was pounding in my ears. I wondered if I would even hear him announce my name over the roar of my heart.

This was it.

"Now, as many of you know, there are plenty of other Crosses out there, living all over the world. But we recently found out there was another Cross out there that we've welcomed into our family with open arms. Last but certainly not least, my niece Raven."

I knew I must have looked unsure of myself, but I couldn't help it. Being in the public eye, let alone being introduced as a member of one of the richest families in this country, wasn't something I was used to. But I shoved my insecurities to the floor as I managed to smile at the crowd and give a small wave as they clapped for me.

There was a slight undertone that seemed to pass through the room. I wasn't surprised and I'm sure there were many questions about who I was and how this had all come to be.

I looked around the room, not focusing on anyone in particular until I saw him.

Nash.

My mouth dropped open before I caught myself. I slammed my mouth shut again as I watched shock register on his face before anger quickly followed. It was the same look that I saw on his face when I returned to Brentson.

I should have known he'd be here. Or at least assumed that he would be.

Preparing for this evening had forced my guard down because I didn't know what I was walking into. I'd thought that once this was done, I could have my phone back and call both Nash and Izzy to tell them what had happened and that I was okay. I didn't want or expect him to find out this way.

Had Kingston known that the Hensons would be here tonight? He should have, since I assumed he was providing security for the event in some capacity, so why hadn't he warned me? I needed to talk to him.

I walked over and was standing on the other side of Ellie as Martin began talking again, wrapping up his introductory speech for the gala. When he was done, the crowd applauded again as we left the stage.

As the Cross family walked over to the two tables that were reserved for us, Kingston, Ellie, and I sat down at one table and were joined by several more people to round out the table. I stuck out my hand to shake everyone's hand and everything was calm and friendly until I reached the last man at the table. He stood up and trained his dark gaze on me.

"Soren," he said.

The man's intimidating stare was enough to force my eyes down. The energy he gave off felt... strange and I couldn't put my finger on why it did. I knew who I was not talking to during this dinner.

But I had bigger problems to deal with. After I sat down in my chair, I looked over to where I knew Nash was sitting just a few feet away and found him staring at me. I quickly turned back around to avoid looking at him.

That did little to change my current problem, however. I

could feel Nash's gaze burning a hole into my back. I couldn't help but wonder what was going through his mind. He'd thought I died days ago and now he knew it had all been a lie.

I ordered a glass of red wine and was thankful when it arrived. My hand shook slightly as I brought the glass of wine to my lips. The urge to throw the glass of wine back was there, but I needed to be mindful of who I was and where I was. Funny how that had changed so much in the last fifteen minutes.

The nerves I'd had earlier? They'd increased tenfold now because I had the extra pressure of not knowing what Nash was thinking or what he might plan to do. Sure there were people around, but there were people around when I was at Elevate too, and he'd found some way to corner me there. Maybe if I could make sure that I wasn't alone with him anywhere, then I could collect my bearings and then reach out to him later so we could discuss this like adults.

There was no chance of that given our history and how tumultuous everything has been since Kingston had blown up one of his own SUV's to give him time to figure out what we needed to do next. Although looking back on it now, I understood why he did what he did, but I wished that things could have been done differently because I knew people were hurt in the process.

At least for the time being, it would look odd for Nash to walk up to me at this table during dinner and with the presentations going on in front of us. Plus, Kingston and Ellie were sitting to my left, so I had them here to stop any confrontations.

But at some point, guests would start dancing and that

would be the perfect opportunity for him to approach me. *Shit.*

I assumed Van Henson wouldn't appreciate Nash causing a scene either. Then again, Nash had no problem causing one at his parents' house during the party they threw...

I shook my head, trying to push those thoughts to the corner of my brain. I didn't need to dwell on it now because it wasn't something I could fix or change right now. Instead, I turned my attention back to the activities on the stage because it was why we were here after all. I took another sip of wine and watched what was unfolding in front of me.

Whoever the Cross family had hired to put this entire event together had done a fantastic job. It was lovely seeing all of the highlights that Cross Industries wanted to share with their guests and with the world. They also gave out awards to not only people who worked for Cross Industries, they gave them out to people who did exceptional work across many fields, and it was one of the ways they gave recognition to people who deserved it.

While what I wanted to do about Nash stayed on my mind, I was able to distract myself from it for the time being. During the event, Kingston left our table and returned just as the last presentation was beginning. When the event wrapped up, I stood up and pulled Kingston to the side while Ellie went to talk to Anais.

"I wanted to ask you something."

"Go for it."

"Why didn't you warn me that Nash was going to be here tonight?"

"Because I didn't think it would be an issue."

I did a double take. "What do you mean you didn't think it

would be an issue? You know what happened the night of the explosion!"

"Telling you that he was going to be here would have done nothing but make you panic."

He was right but that was beside the point. "Still, you took that choice away from me. You should have said something."

Kingston's expression turned serious. "There are some things that you don't know. The number of leads we are following, the number of threats that have just been made against you because of you being brought under the Cross family umbrella. I'm not going to always be able to tell you every little thing that happens."

That made me pause temporarily. "Were you thinking that Nash was a part of the plot to kidnap me?"

"We couldn't be sure, but we've confirmed that he wasn't."

I knew that he hadn't been, but I didn't know that Kingston had him listed as a suspect. "Why didn't you at least tell me that?"

"Because I didn't want to cause you even more pain than you've already had, Raven. He was on our list, and we cleared him."

"Would you have told me if he had been behind all of this?"

Kingston stared at me before nodding his head. At least he was willing to give me that.

"Kingston."

We both turned and found Damien and another man coming over to us. Damien gave me a small smile as he turned his attention to his cousin.

"Can I have a minute? Ben and I want to talk to you about a new security venture."

Kingston nodded and shifted his gaze toward me. "I'll be right back."

He walked away and I turned back to the table I'd been sitting at. I pulled my chair back out and sat down, content to wait until I could leave this place and head back up to my hotel room. I dug into the clutch that I'd decided to use tonight and pulled out the burner phone. I checked the time and wondered if I had enough time to run to the bathroom and redo my lipstick before anyone noticed that I was gone.

"Ah, there you are."

The voice sounded oddly familiar but I couldn't quite place it. I looked over my shoulder and saw that Van Henson was only a few feet away from me. Nash wasn't with him, and I was both relieved and disappointed. It was probably best that we had some space between us right now. But his father had a whole lot of nerve coming up to me after the agreement we'd reached.

"I have nothing to say to you." And I didn't. I'd said everything I wanted to say to him years ago when I left Brentson the first time and I hadn't said a word to him when Nash brought me to their party when I returned.

"I'm not here to cause a scene. I just wanted to talk to you. Briefly."

Of course he wasn't. Because there were too many eyes in the room that would be very interested in what he could be saying to enrage me.

I sighed and turned to face him. I straightened my posture and said, "What can I do for you, Mr. Henson?"

Anyone looking at us would think that Van had the upper hand in this situation, given that I was sitting and he was standing. I could see in his eyes a slight uncertainty as he reflected on my newfound family and status.

It was the first time since this all began that I'd been able to put away my insecurities about myself and start to embrace my strength.

"I wanted to say that I'd like to wipe the slate clean between us. I know that there were some harsh feelings between the two of us, and I wanted to bury the hatchet so to speak."

I folded my arms across my chest, not believing a single word that had come out of his mouth. "Is this because Martin Cross introduced me as his niece earlier tonight? Because you didn't seem to want to bury anything the last time I saw you."

I remembered how poorly Van had treated Nash about me when he didn't know that I was in the next room in the cabin where Nash and I were hiding from the world. It was easy to see that this was a ploy to get into my good graces because if he'd made enemies of the Cross family, it would be an uphill battle for him to climb to get anywhere in this world.

"No. It's because of your relationship with my son."

I pursed my lips, still not believing a word he'd said. First, Nash hadn't told him that he'd thought he had seen me die in a car explosion. Second, there was no way he could think I was buying his bullshit. Then again, he'd always had people around him kissing his ass, so maybe he did think I was falling for every word he said.

"Van, I want nothing to do with you ever and I'd appreciate it if you would find your family and leave me alone." If I hadn't felt the words leave my mouth or heard my voice, I don't know if I would have believed that I'd just said that.

"Our conversation the night when I made you the offer will stay between us, correct?"

I snorted. Too late for that because Nash knew. "Should have made me sign an NDA then."

He looked at me in shock that I knew what that legally binding document was. I could see that I'd made him speechless, probably something that rarely, if ever, happened and I wanted to be the person who literally patted themselves on the back. Doing that in public might look a little weird, so instead, I did it mentally and stood up from the table.

"You're right. I should have. Your mother told me that you were smart and that no matter what stood in your way, you would do everything to fight for what you wanted, including my son."

If he thought that he could distract me by using my mother, he had another thing coming. I made sure to keep my expression blank as I asked, "When did she say this?"

"The night you and Clarissa hosted us for dinner."

I walked up to him, and we were standing side by side, with me facing in the opposite direction as him. "You should have taken her advice because it wasn't a hint. It was a warning. Listen, you should have been more careful with the deals you've made because you never know when they are going to come back to bite you in the ass. I might not have said anything yet publicly about what I know about you, but I always want it to be in the back of your mind that you never know when I'm going to drop that truth bomb. Now, have a good night."

I walked away from him with my head held high and a smirk on my face. It felt amazing to best him and knowing that I now held that over his head made me feel better than I had in quite a while.

I walked out of the ballroom and found Kingston and Damien talking together in a corner of the waiting area. The man that Damien had been walking with when he approached Kingston and me was nowhere to be found.

"Hey," I said and both men turned toward me. "I was going to head back up to my room if there is nothing else we need to do? It's been a long day."

"I think Dad wanted to take a few photos with the whole family before we all left, but other than that..." Damien's voice trailed off as his attention was drawn to something across the room. I looked in the direction he was looking and found him staring at his fiancée, Anais. I had to admit that it was very sweet.

"Okay. I hope we can do it soon before I turn into a pumpkin."

Both men chuckled and Kingston said, "Uncle Martin is waving us over now. Let's take these photos so we can all get out of here."

I followed Kingston and Damien as they walked over to where Martin, Selena, Gage, and Broderick were standing. I pulled out my lipstick and my setting powder and quickly tried to refresh my look so that I wouldn't look like a mess during these photos that would be available for public consumption.

It took a long time to get the photos done because we were taking them in smaller groups first, before the group photo that we all took together. There were also photos that were taken with the Cross men and their partners. Instead of me taking a photo alone when it came to that point, I got to take photos with Kingston. The whole experience capped off a mind-blowing evening as I still couldn't wrap my head around me having no blood relatives and then finding out I had a bigger family than I ever could have imagined.

What concerned me most was that throughout all of this, I hadn't seen Nash since the gala's program was officially over. Had he just left? I wouldn't blame him if I were being honest.

One of Kingston's men took me up to my hotel room. Kingston had told me that the Cross family had rented out the whole floor I was on because so many Cross family members were staying on the same floor. They wanted to take every precaution imaginable to prevent any kind of incident, and I was grateful.

I opened my hotel room door and sighed. The night was finally over, and I could finally take off these shoes. Just opening the door of my room released so much tension that had been building over the course of these last several hours.

I reached over to turn on one of the lights in the room and when I did, I gasped. My hands flew to my mouth as I took in the sight before me. There was no way I was seeing the display in front of me.

19

RAVEN

I t took me several seconds to recover as my heart raced inside my chest. I was too stunned to move. Nash was sitting in a chair near the window, and I was left shocked and confused.

"Close the door, Raven."

Without even thinking about it, I followed his directions and immediately afterward, doubts about doing that sprang to the surface. I could have run out into the hallway and yelled for the guard who had walked me to my room. There was a chance that he was still nearby or standing near the door, right?

I put my hand on the doorknob and Nash shook his head slightly. That simple motion was enough to set my body on fire.

"How did you get in here?"

He stood up and I bit back a curse. I couldn't read the look on his face, so I didn't know what he was thinking. The only thing I had to go on was the shocked, then angry, look on his face.

"Kingston let me in," he said as he took a step toward me. "After we had a little chat during the gala."

I rolled my eyes, thinking back to when Kingston had left our table and to the conversation I had with him earlier. "Of course he did." *Damn traitor.*

"Kingston apparently cleared me of being involved in your kidnapping plot."

I nodded, confirming the news I'd heard from Kingston. It also made me wonder if he'd cleared Van of any involvement either or if the man had even been on his list to begin with. "I wasn't even sure why you were considered a suspect since you killed my would-be kidnapper."

"It would be an excellent way to cover my tracks because I would have killed the only person who could have been able to confirm that I took out the hit."

I hated that he was right. He took another step toward me, closing the distance between us. The room that we were in was a nice size, but it felt as if the walls were growing closer. I was almost willing to bet that the walls around us could have crashed down and it still wouldn't have shifted the intensity that I was getting from Nash.

"You know what Kingston knew?"

I shrugged as I tried to appear unaffected by his presence. Then again, he probably knew that I was lying.

Nash took another step toward me, and it took everything in me to not move back. If I did, I had nowhere to go but a closed door. "He knew how much you wanted to see me."

The look in his eyes was primal. There was an edge to how he was looking at me that sent a sliver of fear through me.

"There is a guard standing outside my hotel room door right now and all it would take is me screaming to—"

"You're not going to do that, are you, Raven?"

He put a special emphasis on my name as he took another step. This time, I did back up and my back hit the door softly. A wicked smile appeared on his lips as I licked mine. He had me right where he wanted me, and he knew it. I was too curious about what he was going to do to open the door and alert any security guards that might be on this floor.

"There's a lot we need to talk about, Little Bird, but right now isn't the time."

"Nash, I can explain—"

My voice faded because of the look on his face. The primal look had shifted for a brief moment and I, once again, had no idea what he was thinking. When he didn't say anything right away, I found myself mentally begging him to say a word, to give me a hint of what was going through his mind. Instead, he stared at me and drew a hand down my cheek.

"I had to make sure that you were real." His words were a punch to the gut that I hadn't been expecting. The softness of his words caressed me, but as soon as the sinister look in his eyes returned, I knew what was going to happen next.

He wanted me. Any barriers in the way of him getting to me had no chance of surviving.

The hand that was resting on my face moved toward my chin and pushed my head up. I was forced to look up at him, into the eyes that had contained my dreams and had haunted my nightmares when I was apart from him.

I trembled slightly before his lips landed on mine. It was a homecoming for the both of us because home for me was wherever he was.

"You know, it's funny how we met again and you're here wearing a very expensive dress. It looks stunning on you, by the way."

I raised an eyebrow. "Do you care about this dress?"

"No. I was just making small talk before I fucked you."

He didn't give me an opportunity to react. His lips slammed onto mine, removing any other thoughts. I'd felt a longing for him since I first saw him as I was standing up on the stage before all of the people who had been invited to the gala, and there was no denying the hold he had on me.

When I saw him at the gala, I knew that my panties were soaked. The mixture of worry and danger had done a number on my body. After hours of me thinking about when he would strike and make his presence known, it had finally come down to this and I was more than ready to take everything that he would throw at me.

I didn't try to fight the pull he had on me. His punishing kiss was ruining the lipstick I'd made an effort to put on just before I took those photos downstairs. I didn't care and it didn't matter. The only thing that did was getting as close to him as possible.

Our tongues danced around one another's as we enjoyed each other's taste after what had been a drought. If I had my way, there would be no more of that and way more of this.

My hands grasped whatever I could grab as I tried to pull Nash as close to me as possible. I could feel the muscles in his shoulders as I shoved his tuxedo jacket off his body. Where it landed in the room, it didn't matter.

Nothing mattered but getting us both naked as quickly as possible.

When he broke our kiss, he took a deep breath and said, "I can't wait to stick my cock in you and fuck you so hard that every time you sit down, you'll think of this moment right here. The moment I fucked you so hard that you begged for mercy."

A groan left my mouth. "That's what I want."

I was surprised I'd voiced the words out loud. It was the second time tonight I'd shocked myself. Maybe I was turning over a new leaf and I couldn't deny that I was absolutely loving it.

It seemed to be what Nash wanted too, because his lips landed on mine again and I was left breathless. When I tried to break away, I swore he growled and tightened his grip on me. The possessiveness he showed made my nipples tighten and I could feel them brushing along the fabric of my strapless bra. When he finally gave me some reprieve, I gasped as I tried to suck in a ton of air. He'd let my lips go, but his hands remained around my waist, holding me close to his body.

This is what I'd been missing. This is what we'd both yearned for.

I put some space between us and let the palms of my hands slide down his chest, allowing myself to once again feel all of the hardness of his muscles beneath my fingers. I reached where the waistband of his pants began and moved lower before he grabbed my wrists in his hand and lifted them up. When he pushed my hands so that he was holding them against the door, I swallowed hard. If this wasn't one of the most erotic things I'd ever experienced, I would be lying to myself.

He glanced up at where our hands met before looking back down at my eyes. "You're still wearing the bracelet."

"Why do you sound surprised? It means the world to me."

The way his eyes studied mine warmed me from the inside out. Not to mention, having to give up control to him and not knowing what he was going to do next was a bigger turn on than I thought it would be. I shifted my legs, allowing him to step between them. He only stayed there for a second before he took a step back and leaned forward. I squealed when he let go of my wrists and pulled me toward him, forcing my body over his shoulder. It reminded me of how he handled me when we were up at his cabin, locked away from the world.

Nash carried me for several seconds before he unceremoniously tossed me on the bed, and I found myself staring up at him. The man before me was so handsome it almost hurt. When he ran a hand through his dirty-blond hair, I wished it was my fingers entangled in his strands. That would provide enough leverage for me to keep him right where I wanted him: on his knees with his mouth on my pussy.

It seemed as if he had the same idea as me because he dropped to his knees, and I felt him lift up my dress before moving his head so that he was no longer visible. It reminded me of what a groom might do when he was getting the garter from the bride.

I felt light caressing from his fingertips as he made his way up to the thong I'd thought was a good idea to wear under this gown. It had to be drenched and he was getting a face full of my excitement for any journey we were going to be on tonight. My hands made their way to my breasts. I shoved the top of my dress and my strapless bra down so that

I could play with my nipples. I squirmed under his touch as he ran a finger up and down my panty-covered slit.

The anticipation he was building within me was going to make me combust. If he didn't touch me where I wanted him, I didn't know what I was going to do. As if he'd known what I was thinking, I felt him shift my thong to the side. I waited with bated breath for him to touch me. But he didn't. Well, not exactly.

I felt his breath on my already sensitive clit, and I shivered in response. I looked down and all I could see was a small bump where his head was resting between my legs. When he blew on me again, I jumped, and I heard his dark chuckle fill the room. He knew he was driving me wild and clearly didn't give a fuck.

"Nash," I moaned, and his chuckling stopped. I didn't have a hint of what he might be thinking because I couldn't see his face. But then I felt his fingers playing near my entrance and he wasted no more time before sliding one of his fingers in.

My head flew back in relief. He'd finally given me what I wanted. I could die happy now.

His tongue joined the party, and I fought the urge to squeeze my thighs together. This was the homecoming I'd deserved.

Since I couldn't watch what he was doing, the only senses I could rely on were hearing the sounds that he made while licking my pussy and feeling the way that he was touching me. Not being able to watch him forced my other senses into overdrive as my eyes drifted closed, determined to enjoy every second of this. It was only a matter of time before my body was going to turn into a quivering mess as I recovered from every sensation he was taking my body through.

"More. I want more," I said as the pressure within me continued to build.

Instead of responding verbally, he added another finger to my pussy, and I nearly screamed. The intensity was increasing, and it became more difficult to control my body. Every emotion flowed through me, causing much confusion. The only thing that made sense was what Nash was doing to my pussy right now.

I played with my nipples harder, determined to reach my orgasm as quickly as possible. I felt Nash's mouth pull away from me and with that his fingers fucked me harder, giving me exactly what I wanted when I needed it. My body sailed out of control as I started to go over the edge. As I groaned, Nash put his mouth back on me as he began to lick the fruits of his labor.

As I tried to recover, he lifted my gown up so that I could see him now. He watched me as his finger began to move toward my ass before he said, "No one has fucked you here."

He spoke it as if he knew versus him asking me. Still, I shook my head.

Nash's grin made him look happy and wicked at the same time. "Looks like I'll be the one taking your virginity here too."

"Wait a minute—"

The smile left his face and he'd turned serious. "Not now, but it will be something we work toward."

He waited for my response, and I could see him wondering if I was going to be opposed to doing something like that. When I showed no further hesitation on my end, he groaned. "That's my fucking girl."

I didn't have an opportunity to overthink his words because he was on the move. I watched as he stood up. While my mind wanted to sit there and just watch whatever he was going to do while I recovered, my body had other plans.

I leaned up to undo his pants and he stepped out of my reach.

"While I would love to fuck your mouth, it's been too long since I've had you. All my cock wants is to sink into that wet pussy of mine. Take off the dress."

I shivered involuntarily as goose bumps appeared on my flesh. Nash had the ability to do that with just a few words. When I'd thought he'd made a mistake calling my pussy his, the look in his eyes said nothing of the sort. He'd meant every word.

Mine.

It was such a powerful word and while my gut reaction might have been to argue with him, I couldn't deny that his saying that word made me wetter.

He moved out of my way so that I could stand up and unzip the dress while he removed his clothes.

"You don't know how fucking hot you look right now with your perfect hairstyle completely messed up and your bra doing anything but keeping your breasts contained. You look as if you don't give a fuck what anyone thinks."

I undid my bra and removed my thong before I said, "The only thing I care about is us fucking tonight."

He smirked and I knew that, once again, it was game time. "That can be arranged."

With us both naked outside of the jewelry I had on and the high heels I'd worn to the gala, he pushed me back onto the bed and settled between my legs once more. The moment of truth was here, and I was more than ready for it.

"Play with your nipples."

"Again?" There was a hint of sassiness in my voice and it made Nash's lips twitch.

"Were you playing with them when I was fucking you with my tongue?"

"Yes, I was," I said confidently.

"Did I say you could do that?"

The seriousness in his voice forced my eyes to widen. But no words ever left my mouth to respond to him. He used that moment of shock to slide into me. There was no doubt in my mind that I was utterly and completely his.

"Fuck," I heard him mumble under his breath and he pulled back and then thrust forward into my pussy. The pleasure that ran through my veins was starting to grow and I was more than ready for another orgasm courtesy of Nash Henson.

His thrusts became a steady rhythm, and I was more than willing to surrender to his touch. Based on the sweat that was forming just above his brow, I could see that Nash was giving me everything he had. It was as if he was fucking me so that he was able to brand me, showing everyone that I was his and he was mine. I couldn't care less about what he was doing as long as it meant another orgasm being given to my body.

He pumped into me twice more and I reached down and touched my clit because I was so close. He growled at the sight, and I waited for him to say that he didn't give me permission to do that, but he didn't. Good, because I had no intention of stopping.

I found myself alternating between moaning and screaming as my climax came crashing through me. After the day I'd had, there was no way I was going to be able to stay up longer than a few minutes after that last orgasm. What made it even better was that Nash didn't stop pumping into me. He hadn't had his own orgasm yet and he was determined to get it.

The more he pounded into me, the more sensitive I felt as I rode out my orgasm. He thrust into me two more times before he let out a loud groan as he joined me on the other side of nirvana.

He took several deep breaths as he looked down at me. He slowly moved his hips and then he said, "I was going to regret not telling you this for the rest of my life if I hadn't seen you again. Look at me."

My eyes sprung open, bringing me out of the lust-filled haze I'd been in. I'd wanted to stay in this orgasmic bliss forever.

"I love you."

Tears immediately pooled near the corner of my eyes. My breath was caught in my throat as I tried to find a way to release the tightness in my chest. This couldn't be real, could it?

When he removed himself from my body, I knew that, without a doubt, this was real because I felt the loss of him immediately. I knew that we had a lot of healing to do with everything that had happened, but at least right now, we were connected. We were one.

Before he left the bed, I whispered loud enough for him to hear, "I love you too."

I meant every word.

He squeezed my hand before heading into the bathroom. Just that small touch, combined with what we'd just experienced, made everything brighter. All I ever wanted was to be with him in every way imaginable. He was the only one who could make me feel this way.

He brought back two washcloths and cleaned us both up before he lay back down in the bed. He pulled me toward him until I lay on his chest.

I tried to force myself to stay awake. It was out of fear that he might leave my hotel room and I'd never see him again. He'd said he loved me, and deep down, I suspected that he wouldn't leave, but until we talked and had more clarity, the weight on my chest was still there. It felt as if it was something I deserved and now I was starting to understand how much it crushed him.

20

NASH

Her soft breaths were all I heard as I lightly ran my hand up and down her arm. Just this little action was one of the small things I missed when I thought I'd lost her forever. It was something that I'd taken for granted when we were in high school and hadn't gotten nearly enough chances to do after she returned and before Kingston decided that the best course of action here was to star in his very own summer blockbuster movie.

I could barely make fun of what had happened now, and it was only because she was back in my arms, resting after the havoc I'd caused her body.

It was cute to watch her fight sleep, but eventually sleep won out. I knew I should join her, but for some reason I couldn't. Instead, I was lost in my own thoughts about this entire situation as I tried to make sense of everything that occurred.

Deep down, that was the only thing that mattered, even if I wanted to go and fuck up Kingston's entire existence for putting me through the turmoil that he had. Part of me wondered if that had been a test to see how I would react to her being taken from me once more, but I knew the focus was on finding whoever wanted to harm her, and quickly.

Still, the fact that he'd had me listed as a suspect up until tonight pissed me off, even if the logical part of my brain told me it made sense until he could clear my name. After all, everyone who'd ever been around me knew that I'd hated her for what she did for years, not knowing that my father had been the reason for it.

I tried to brush that aside before anger took over all of my emotions. It would do no good dwelling on it now, but it did make me wonder if my father had anything to do with any of this.

He for sure wouldn't have wanted to bring Raven back to Brentson because she knew at least one of his secrets. But the rest of it? I hated to say that it was definitely possible.

My father was a skilled politician who could reframe just about anything so that you'd see his point of view and could talk his way out of anything. I thought I would have been able to tell if he'd gone this far out of his way to harm Raven. Now he'd have to worry about whether it would get out that he'd attempted to kidnap one of the heirs of the Cross family fortune. That would be great for his political ambitions.

I needed to talk to Kingston more about what he'd found and if it resulted in him drawing any conclusions. The brief conversation he and I had didn't include much on that front and we needed to get to the bottom of this.

But for now, I would enjoy having her in my arms, a feeling that I'd missed immensely. It had been less than a couple of weeks since the car explosion, but it felt like an eternity.

It had been just as long since I'd felt any sense of peace. It had only come with the connection she and I had made while at the cabin that had slowly morphed into... something that hadn't had much time to develop once we were back in the outside world again. The urge to go back in time to change what had happened was there, but I couldn't. Nor would I if I could.

I snuggled in as close as I could without disturbing her. She shifted her body slightly when I moved but didn't make a motion to hint that she was waking up. I leaned over and pressed the button that would turn all of the lights off in the room.

Before I could think about anything else, I settled into a deep sleep.

I BEGAN to wake up when I felt Raven stirring beside me. Her head was still resting on my chest with her hand resting beside it. The curtains were drawn so it was still pitch black in the bedroom, although the clock on the nightstand beside me said that it was eight in the morning.

"Nash?"

Her voice was still raspy with sleep, and it was one of the sexiest things I'd ever heard.

"I'm going to turn the light on."

"Okay."

I reached over and felt around until my fingers touched what I assumed was the button to turn on the lights. When I pressed it, light immediately filled the room, and I looked down at Raven who was squinting from the change in our environment.

"I warned you that I was going to turn the lights on."

"I know, and I still wasn't prepared."

I chuckled as she moved off of my chest and I immediately missed the warmth that having her up against me had brought to my body. She'd gripped the blanket to keep parts of her body hidden, but when she reached up to stretch, the covers fell, giving me ample opportunity to stare at her breasts. If my cock hadn't been hard already, that would have easily done the trick.

When she grabbed for the blanket again to cover herself, I raised an eyebrow. "I saw plenty of you last night and all of the other nights we had sex, Raven."

"It's chilly in here."

"Okay, as long as that's the only reason you're hiding yourself away from me." There was a chance she was cold, but the blush on her cheeks made me wonder if she was being shy.

She cuddled up next to me again, adjusting her body so that she was resting her head on my shoulder this time.

We lay like that for a couple of minutes before she spoke. "We have a lot to talk about."

"Normally that would make many people panic, but in this case, I completely agree."

"Where should we begin?"

"Personally, I want to talk about what happened the night of the car explosion and then more about what deal you had with my father."

"Why does it suddenly feel like it's way too early to talk about any of this?"

"Because neither one of us actually wants to talk about any of this, but in order to move past it, we need to."

She looked up at me with a quizzical look on her face. "I've always known you were smart, but when did you become wise?"

Her question made me remember the Chevalier task I had coming up. I hadn't done anything to prepare for the task that would determine whether or not I had adopted some of the qualities that were found in the Chevaliers who were owls. "Fuck..."

"What's wrong?"

"I have some Chevalier stuff I should be prepping for, but I don't want to do it anymore."

A look of concern passed over her features. "Does this have anything to do with the chairmanship?"

Had I made a mistake and mentioned something to her about it? "What do you know about that? Did I—"

She shook her head no. "Not much, but I did meet the chairman of the New York City Chevaliers the other day."

"You did? You met Parker?"

She nodded this time. "Parker Townsend, right?"

I didn't doubt that she had, but that confirmed her story. There more than likely wouldn't be another reason why she'd know his name because I was pretty sure that him being chairman wasn't public knowledge, although it wasn't being hidden either.

"And what did he say?" I asked and waited for her response as if my life depended on it.

"That he was the reason why I was brought back to Brentson."

I did a double take before staring at her. Our conversation

wasn't sticking to the topics we'd agreed to talk about, but it was bringing up other things that clearly, we needed to discuss. And it seemed as if everything she was saying was shocking, to say the least.

I was starting to draw connections to things, but I wasn't sure if I was being presumptuous or not. To me, it had been obvious that she'd been brought back to Brentson to be listed as something I needed to conquer, but was I right? "Did it have anything to do with the chairmanship trials that were taking place at Brentson?"

"Yeah. He brought me back here because he wanted me to be some sort of test for you. And he did it by promising to tell me more about what happened to my mother. Like how she died and all of that."

My assumption was correct, but before I could respond, she continued.

"Is whatever is happening between us a part of that or is this real?"

"Do you mean our relationship? This is the most real thing in my life. Especially right now. Don't doubt that what I feel for you is real. I never stopped loving you, even when I thought I hated you."

I could see that she was about to cry, but I meant every word.

When the first tear fell, I used my thumb to immediately wipe it up. I didn't want to be the one responsible for her tears, but the most I could wish for right now was that they were tears of happiness.

"You don't know how much I wished over the years that I would hear you say something like that. Wow. I'm just surprised at how emotional it made me."

More tears began to fall, and I did my best to keep up with them. I reached over and grabbed a tissue and wiped the wetness on her face before she took over, and I pulled her closer to me in an effort to soothe her. After a few moments, she pulled away and I watched as she pushed the hair that had fallen out of her updo away from her face. Then she reached up and touched the back of her head with one hand.

"Fuck, I didn't take my hair down last night."

"We were quite busy so that's understandable."

It was then that her lips twitched, and I knew she was fighting a grin. I'd achieved my goal of vanquishing the tears from her eyes. When she started to giggle, I held my breath as I tried not to laugh. When her giggles grew louder, it became harder to compose myself. All control went out the window when she let out a full-on belly laugh.

I joined her in her laughter, but I forced myself to quiet my own chuckles so I could enjoy the sounds of her happiness.

"Okay, okay," she said as she tried to catch her breath. "We need to get back to our conversation."

"Yes. So you met Parker, and he told you he brought you back here because you needed to be here for the trials. What did he tell you about your mother?"

"Well, I learned that my father killed my mother."

If there was any way for the mood in the room to make a one-eighty turn, that was the way to do it.

"I'm so sorry to hear that." I didn't know what else I could say to make things better.

"I mean, it was a shock, but I feel more at peace with having closure. I always thought there was more to the story than what I was being told and to be able to get that closure was a big deal to me. I had a few days to sit there with the news and just take it in before admitting it to you, which is probably why I haven't dissolved into tears again. You know what the kicker was?"

"What's that?"

"My mom did all of it for me. She told Neil that he needed to come clean to me about being my father because I deserved to know. She told him that if he didn't do it, she was going to finally tell me. Based on the date of the letter, it was a couple of weeks before she was killed."

"That's absolutely horrible."

"Yeah, if he wasn't already dead, I would be tempted to..."

Her voice trailed off and I didn't try to do anything to fill the temporary silence that passed between the two of us.

Raven cleared her throat, and I said, "Let's talk about the car explosion."

"I didn't know anything about what was going on until it happened."

I'd figured as much; unless Kingston had found a way to contact her beforehand and she hadn't told me, there was no way for her to have known.

"I was walking right behind you, and he split us up on purpose in order to get me into one of his other vehicles, which would then drive ahead so that they could blow up the one that was supposedly carrying you and him."

Raven nodded and then said, "Yeah. He did tell me the plan once I was in the SUV in order to make sure that I knew what to do when the time came. He instructed me to dart out of the SUV and run as far away from it as I could."

"And during that time, I was being hit on my head with a gun by Landon."

Her eyes narrowed slightly before they widened. "Landon hit you?"

I gave her a quick rundown of what had happened after Landon had knocked me out cold and watched the range of emotions that passed along her face. It was as if she'd been there when it happened. Her ability to empathize with people was one of the things I loved about her.

"And you saw him tonight?"

"I did. Did you?"

She shook her head. "To be honest, I was so focused on my introduction and then on you when I saw you that I hadn't thought to look for him. Even after him coming with Kingston to my house before everything happened."

"What happened to you after the car explosion?"

Raven swallowed hard. "Kingston found me and we hiked through the woods before we reached another car. He drove me to an apartment in the city and I stayed there until I got to this hotel room tonight. It is absolutely stunning. I've been doing coursework whenever I could there too."

At least Kingston had taken care of her and that made me connect the dots with President Caldwell too. He more than likely knew about this arrangement and was hesitant to comment on it for fear of leaking something he shouldn't.

"You also wanted to talk more about the deal with your father." She closed her eyes and didn't say a word for a minute. "There's not much you don't know about it. He paid me to leave, and I did, and in return, I kept my mouth shut about him being in a madam's little black book. However, he did talk to me at the gala; I assume it was after you'd already made your way up here."

My hold on her tightened before I realized that I was

squeezing her too hard. I didn't like her interacting with my father when I wasn't there, especially when he had everything to lose if she did speak. "What did he say?"

She quickly told me what happened between her and my father and I almost clapped because of how she handled her interaction with him.

"I do think you're right. He is trying to smooth things over because he knows that now I connect him to the Cross family. I'm sure it's only a matter of time before he starts trying to kiss my ass."

Just as Raven was about to say something else, her stomach growled. "And now I'm starving, so whatever else we need to talk about, can we do it after breakfast?"

Who was I to deny her? "Breakfast first, fucking next, and then we can talk more if you wish. Deal?"

The blush on her cheeks told me that I'd hit the jackpot.

21

RAVEN

"I don't want to move," I said as I took another sip of the coffee in front of me. It was tasty, but nothing compared to what I had at the apartment during the time I was supposed to be "dead."

Nash and I were enjoying a lovely breakfast after finally climbing out of bed and ordering room service. I'd thrown on a pair of pajamas that I'd brought with me, and Nash was sitting in nothing but boxers. It made our meal more exciting for me as I took the opportunity to steal glances at his body while we ate our eggs, bacon, and pancakes. This might be a typical start to the morning for many people around the world, but I didn't want to take it for granted because there were so many reasons why we shouldn't be here right now. Enjoying this meal with one another felt like a privilege, not a guarantee, and I did my best to soak the entire moment in.

"This is so peaceful."

"Cross Sentinel booked every room on this floor as a way to lock it down in order to protect the family members who wanted to stay onsite versus traveling to and from the event."

It felt weird being in the know about things like this and all that the Cross family would do to protect their own. It definitely would take some getting used to.

"Is the reason why they locked down this floor because of you?"

"Eh. There are apparently a lot of threats against the Cross family in general and Kingston thought that the gala would be a big enough event where someone might try something because of the audience they would have and the publicity that would come afterward. But as far as I know, nothing happened."

"Well, that's not a bad thing."

"Right, but we still don't know who is doing all of this against me and why. It's easy to write some of the other threats off as minor or not likely to happen due to x, y, z, but there is a real threat against me and we still don't know who is behind it."

"Which has frustrated me like no other. I spent most of the last few days after the explosion trying to find out who was behind all of this, but I didn't have much luck. At least we have some answers, like Parker being the one who brought you here and paid for your tuition, so it's definitely not him. Could it be someone who hated Neil Cross and decided to take it out on you?"

"Could be, but this feels more personal."

Nash rubbed his hand along his chin before reaching for his glass of orange juice. "It also doesn't explain the text messages I've been getting."

I thought back to just before I rolled out of the car in an effort to escape Nash. "Or that we received that particular text message at the same time."

"Right. Something else is going on here and it seems as if it involves both of us versus just me. Wouldn't it make more sense that way?"

"Or they have something against me and are using you as a way to get back at me."

That thought hung in the air as Nash and I continued eating our breakfast. I noted how much the mood in the room had shifted but didn't want that to weigh too heavily on me right now. It was a huge burden to carry around, but I also wanted to keep in mind that this was supposed to be about Nash and me reuniting and not us solely being concerned about what was going on in the outside world.

I picked up my fork and looked down at my plate while I pushed my food around aimlessly. "While I still have a bad feeling about all of this, Nash, can we switch topics? I've spent most of the last few days alone thinking about everything that was uncovered recently, and it didn't exactly leave me with rosy feelings all over."

"Understandable. I want to talk about what's going to happen when we get back to campus."

I slowly lifted my gaze to meet his, except he wasn't looking at my face. I followed his gaze and noticed that he was staring at the slight gap between the buttons on my shirt, giving him a sneak peek of my breasts.

I swallowed hard. "What do you think is going to happen when we get back to campus?"

His gaze lazily made its way from my chest to look into my eyes. "I want you to move in with me."

I laughed for a second before my laughter died on my lips because of the look on his face. "You can't be serious."

But it was clear he wasn't joking.

"Nash, we can't go from being enemies to moving in together in a matter of weeks. I'm staying in my place because I have a lease."

"Break it."

"It's not as simple as that. I'm on the hook for paying my portion of the rent."

"But it is. You can easily pay your portion of the rent now. Hell, you could pay the whole rent for the rest of the year."

I rolled my eyes, even though he had a good point. I decided to use a different approach. "Why should I move in with you? Make your case."

"Because we can wake up like we did today, every morning."

"You fight dirty." I'd enjoyed waking up with him as much as he obviously had, but that didn't mean I was ready to move in with him.

Nash's smirk heated me to my core, and I hoped that I could contain the warmth from showing up on my cheeks.

"But back to why you should move in with me, I have a doorman and we have security on site that would at least make it safer than the house you live in now."

"I'm sure Kingston would have no issue having an increased presence near my house in order to keep me safe."

"But is that something you want? Having someone watch your every move?"

I shrugged. "It wouldn't be much different than what's going on now. I already feel as if I live in a fishbowl ninety percent of the time anyway."

Why was I even having this debate with him? He'd only entered my life weeks ago and had no problem trying to run it the way he saw fit.

"I'm not going to move in with you and if you love me like you say you do, you'll respect my decision."

Nash stared back at me, but his expression remained hidden. Not even a small hint was visible. Although his stare made me slightly uncomfortable, I wasn't taking back my statement. Moving in with him right now wasn't the right move for us. Plus, if the person was only after me, I was putting his life at risk by living with him.

"You know I respect you."

There was a "but" there, but whether or not he was willing to share what he was now thinking was another matter altogether.

"Let's come to a compromise."

"I didn't know you knew the meaning of the word."

Nash tapped my foot under the table, relieving the tension from our current conversation.

"I apologize. What do you think would make a good compromise?"

"You stay over at my apartment some nights per week with me and I stay over at your place with you. It's not exactly living together, but it is something that is bound to happen organically anyway. Kingston's guys can do whatever they need to protect you. If things change for a few days and we need to be apart, then so be it, but you'll still have your security team in place to help ward off any threats."

I tossed around the idea in my head a few times. I wouldn't have an official answer right away, but it wasn't a half-baked plan. Having Nash there would provide some much-needed reassurance in my life, but I still didn't like that this idea might be putting his life at risk. Then again, he had no issue with murdering anyone who tried to harm me, so he clearly didn't have an issue with defending himself.

"Fine. I can compromise on that plan as long as everyone is okay with you staying over several times during the week. Have you heard from Izzy at all? Kingston said they were doing well, but I suspect that my not being there for days would have raised some red flags."

Nash shook his head. "Haven't heard from her at all. I wonder what Kingston told her to not have her freaking out about you?"

Add that question to the ever-growing list of things I wanted answers to.

I placed my fork next to my plate and grabbed the napkin on my lap. "I'm done eating and I think I'm going to take a shower."

"Okay."

Nash said nothing else as I stood up, but I could feel his eyes on me as I left the room. I walked into the bathroom and closed the door behind me. I walked over to the sink and grabbed my toothbrush, thinking that this was a great time to brush my teeth. I took my time and as I was rinsing my mouth out, I looked into the mirror and caught Nash's reflection staring back at me.

I turned the faucet off and spun around to face him head-on. That was all it took for Nash to act.

His long stride allowed him to reach me quickly and his lips were on mine before I could blink. Our kiss went from light to intense as Nash's hands made their way into my hair.

He grasped my hair near the nape of my neck and pulled, forcing my face to look up at him. He didn't give me an opportunity to take another breath before claiming my lips with his own.

Nash's other hand landed on my stomach before making its way up to my breast. I assumed that taking the time to unbutton my pajama shirt would have wasted too much energy and time for him so he decided to take the easy route.

I could feel his cock growing harder by the second against my thigh. He was as turned on by this kiss as I was. My hands itched to hold his dick, play with him like he was playing with me, but that was apparently not on the agenda.

Nash loosened the hold he had on my hair until he let go, letting my dark strands fall where they may. When he removed his hand from my breast, I almost whined. I never whined. I wasn't prepared for the loss of his touch, and the effect that he had on me had me thinking and doing things that I wouldn't normally do.

But that was all a part of his plan.

Nash looked down at my shirt as if it had offended him before grasping it and pulling. Thankfully, the shirt was somewhat flimsy, so he didn't rip any buttons or the fabric. He didn't do much damage other than taking it off me and throwing it somewhere in the bathroom.

With me completely topless, he grasped my breast again, but this time focusing on my nipple as he pulled it into his mouth. I watched as he licked and sucked on my nipple, drawing it to a hardened pebble and making me want to curse and beg at the same time. My mind struggled with the decision about whether to grip the counter or run my fingers through his hair. The latter won out, and my fingers found their way into his dirty-blond hair, anchoring his head to my chest.

A low groan left his lips as my fingers massaged his scalp. The idea inspired him because he drew one of his hands down and began playing with the waistband of my pajama shorts.

"Please," I said, but it came out as more of a soft moan.

He stopped licking my nipple and said, "Please what, Little Bird?"

Those four words made me shiver all over even though my body had heated up as a result of his touch and his kiss. What he was doing to me should have been criminal.

"Please... please fuck me with your fingers."

His eyes flashed at my words. It seemed as if I wasn't the only one who was teetering on the edge of control.

He yanked down the pajama shorts that I had on and looked into my eyes as he ran a finger up and down my slit. I mentally dared him to touch me, to fuck me like I knew we both wanted, but he decided to surprise me.

He sank down onto his knees and grabbed my leg. I held on to the counter as he kissed his way from my ankle all the way to my inner thigh. When he was done there, Nash peppered kisses along my other thigh, making sure to skip over the place I wanted him most.

"I thought you were going to give me what I wanted?" My voice sounded slightly deeper and thick with arousal.

"When did I ever say that?"

I could hear a teasing lilt in his voice. He had me right where he wanted me, and he knew it.

"Nash, I—" The rest of my sentence didn't leave my mouth because he'd chosen that exact moment to lift my leg again and place it on his shoulder. He stared at the newfound view of my pussy before he made his move.

This new angle changed things up for me considerably, and I couldn't believe the sensations flying through my body at rapid speed. My hands found their rightful place back in his hair as he licked and teased my clit. He grabbed my ass with both of his hands, forcing my body slightly forward. It angled me in such a way that it gave him even more access to my pussy.

One hand then kept me in place while the other stayed near my ass, massaging it as he made me unravel right before our very eyes.

For a moment, I wondered what he was going to do with the hand touching my ass, but when he moved his hand so that it could join in on the fun, I was overjoyed.

"Fuck," I said as I felt him slide one finger into my pussy. There was no way I was going to survive this onslaught from him.

"Fuck is right. I love how wet you get for me, Little Bird."

He wasn't wrong. There was something about him and about us that made everything just feel right.

When another finger joined the party, I almost felt as if I too, were going to fall to my knees. But Nash made sure that I was steady, and I loved him even more for it. I didn't want anything to get in the way of this orgasm that felt as if it was about to wreck my body.

And I couldn't wait.

I could feel the wave starting and I let out a loud moan. "I'm going to come."

Nash lifted his head and said, "That's it, Little Bird. Come all over my tongue. I want to lick up every drop."

The pressure in my core reached its peak as he got back

into position. It would only take a little bit more before I was...

The thought died as I came hard. My eyes slammed shut and I swear I was seeing stars behind my eyelids. My screams bounced off of the walls of the bathroom and it felt as if my body was just coming down from the highest of highs.

Nash did what he said he was going to do and then some. When I opened my eyes and looked down, I found him staring back at me. The heat in his eyes hadn't dimmed one bit, and I knew that this was far from over. He didn't remove his fingers from me until I'd finished riding out my orgasm.

Nash let my leg down before standing up. He put his fingers up to my lips, coating my lips in my own juices before I opened my mouth, allowing him to slip both fingers inside. I sucked on his fingers and his only response was a low groan.

But I hadn't been prepared for what was next.

Nash pulled his fingers out of my mouth. He then turned me around and the front of my body was leaning up against the bathroom counter and its cold surface immediately began to cool my warm body. The stark difference between the temperature of my body and of the counter made me gasp.

He leaned forward and whispered, "Are you ready to take all of my cock?"

All I could do was nod because I didn't trust myself to say anything useful. I thought the only sounds I could make would be animalistic in nature and it wouldn't answer his question.

Or hell, maybe it would.

"I can't wait to give you every single inch. Bend over and grab hold of the counter."

I did as he asked and waited to see what he would do next. He did something unexpected again.

He spanked my ass, and I jumped before crying out in shock.

When he did it to the other cheek, I was better prepared and instead of it being a surprise, the need for him to do it again and again grew.

When he spanked me a third time, I could have sworn that my eyes rolled into the back of my head. As if he'd heard my inner thoughts, he slapped my ass again and again.

Nash massaged both of my butt cheeks and said, "You don't know how pretty your ass looks right now, Little Bird."

"You don't know how much I want you to fuck me right now."

"Is that so?" Nash ran a hand down my slit, and I stared at Nash through the mirror and watched as a smirk formed on his lips.

"Very much so."

Nash didn't waste any more time. There was no pretense and no more encouragement was needed. He placed a hand on my waist and tapped his cock on my ass a couple of times before he thrust himself into me, making me cry out in pleasure.

This was what I wanted. This was what I'd been waiting for.

"That's right, baby." His voice came out gruff and filled with lust. "You don't know how stunning you look."

But I did. I was staring at the two of us in the mirror and the scene was beautiful. I watched as Nash stared at where our bodies connected, as if he was in a trance. When he shifted his eyes and met mine through the mirror, the smirk was nowhere to be found. Instead, his eyes roamed over my face, studying every inch of it to watch the effect he was having on me.

It wouldn't take much for him to realize what he was doing to me. When he moved his hips faster, I was forced to grip the counter harder because I didn't want to fall. At this point, I was pretty sure I'd forgotten my own name.

What I wanted to do felt risky, but I needed to take the chance because this was feeling way too fucking good. I reached my hand down to play with my pussy. The entire time, our gazes never wavered. The electricity between us was overwhelming, but I refused to look away.

"While you play with your clit, I'm going to play with this. Don't stop until I tell you to."

Nash reached around and played with my nipple and that did it. The pressure that had been building up inside of me finally released.

I found myself screaming again. "Oh. My. Nash!"

"That's exactly what I want to hear."

The orgasm snatched everything within me, and I found myself slinking forward as I tried to recover.

"Did I tell you to stop?" Nash slowed his thrusts and pinched my nipple. "Put your fingers back on your clit."

"I don't think I can come again." My statement came out between haggard breaths as I tried to summon some energy.

I did as he demanded, and he grunted as he picked up the pace again. I didn't think I had the ability to come again, but it was obvious that he was determined to prove that wrong.

And prove me wrong, he did, because I soon felt myself coming on his cock once more.

"Fuck, yes," he mumbled just before he found his release as well.

The whole thing felt like an out-of-body experience. A very tiring out-of-body experience. Nash reached around and held me. I assumed that he too questioned whether I could stand on my own two feet.

He pulled me up so that I was standing, removing his cock from my body. I turned around and leaned on him, not caring about anything else other than trying to catch my breath.

Nash bent down and whispered in my ear, "Now, let's take a bath because there is no way you're going to be able to stand up right now."

22

RAVEN

I glanced at the vanity and thought about what we'd just done. There was no way I would ever be able to look at a bathroom counter the same again and I didn't regret it at all. After our bath together, I felt relaxed and rejuvenated and ready to take on the rest of the day.

I tightened the belt on my robe as I glanced over at Nash, who was busy tying a towel around his waist. When he looked up at me, the look he gave me forced me to shake my head.

"Nope. I know what you're thinking. Nope, nope, nope! We need to get dressed and I need to pack. You need to go back to your hotel and do the same."

"I'm not letting you out of my sight, Raven."

The way he said the words screamed possessive and I couldn't decide how I felt about it. His being overprotective made sense, given the circumstances, and I appreciated his being caring and wanting to ensure my safety. But I'd been on my own for so long that having me "not leave his sight" felt like too much, even though I wanted to spend as much time as I could with him too.

"Nash..."

"If you're going to argue about it with me, it's pointless. I have all of that taken care of."

I sighed. It wasn't worth it, and we had more important things to talk about and do. "Fine."

Without looking to see what his reaction was, I walked out of the bathroom and toward my suitcase, which lay open on my bed.

As I was undoing my robe, I heard Nash leave the bathroom, but I didn't bother turning around to see what he was doing. I let the robe slip off my shoulders and grabbed my bra that I'd laid out on the bed. I only looked over my shoulder when I felt Nash's stare. He was standing directly behind me, his eyes studying the skin I'd just revealed.

I thought about teasing him, but responsibility shined through the lust-filled fog that wanted to take over my brain. Then he left a kiss on my shoulder and walked over to the other side of the bed.

He'd had some clothes for him delivered to the hotel so that he wouldn't have to worry about wearing his tuxedo again. We changed in silence but stole glances at one another every once in a while. I couldn't help but grin because all of this felt so good. Being with him and doing normal things like eating breakfast or taking a bath together was so damn good.

There was still a lot we didn't know about what our futures would look like, but right now, I didn't care because I'd been waiting for a moment like this for so long. I'd spent the last two years mostly alone and lonely, and now I felt anything but.

A sound came from the nightstand, and I reached over and grabbed the burner phone. I knew it could be a text message from only one person since no one else had this phone number.

Kingston: *I'll be at your room shortly.*

Nash cleared his throat, and I looked up at him, but he wasn't looking at my face. He was staring at my wrist.

"I still can't believe that you're still wearing it."

I smiled because Nash was talking about the bracelet again. He was fastening the lock so that I could wear it again after the bath we'd taken. "I am because I love it. Not sure why you're still shocked that I have it on. You didn't do anything that would make me want to take it off and toss it into the Hudson, never to be seen or heard from again."

As I stuffed my heels into my suitcase, Nash said, "Plenty of people would be curious about who gave it to you."

I shrugged. "I don't care what other people think about it."

"It shows the world that you're mine."

I looked him right in the eye and said, "It doesn't if people have to ask questions about it, Nash. This isn't like an engagement ring or a wedding band. And I'm not yours."

"It's the precursor to it. I'm not saying anytime soon, but I don't see my future without you in it."

There was no hiding my surprise and my eyes widened as realization hit me in the face. His comment had been completely unexpected but something I'd longed to hear.

"Even after all of"—I paused as I tried to find the right word—"this?"

"Yes." He took a step toward me, and it reminded me of last night. The connection we shared last night and right now as he was staring deep into my eyes was the same, yet different. "Do you think I would be willing to let you go now that I have you back? All any of this told me is that we can weather anything that will get thrown at us."

I slowly nodded my head. "That's true. And we've had a lot of shit tossed our way."

"And yet, you're right here where you belong. With me."

I couldn't help but grin. His compliments since we'd been reunited again had wrapped me up in a warm embrace that I never wanted to lose again. He walked over to me and lifted my chin so that I was looking up at him. His lips descended on mine and allowed the feeling of his touch to wash over me. When I felt his hands start to make their way toward my shirt, I grabbed hold of them and gently pushed them away.

"I have to check out. Kingston said that he would be here shortly."

"He didn't say when and I didn't get nearly enough of you yet."

He gave me a quick peck this time and I smiled against his lips. I needed to finish up what I was doing but taking a few precious seconds to enjoy what we had wouldn't be the end of the world.

I placed a hand on his chest and gently pushed him away. "He said shortly, and I assumed that meant—"

When there was a knock on the door, we took a step back from one another. I immediately missed the feeling of his touch. Nash put his hand out as if to say wait, and he walked over to the door and looked through the peephole. He turned to look at me and nodded as his hand reached for the door-knob. That must have meant that it was Kingston.

Nash opened the door and in walked Kingston. He acknowledged Nash with a dip of his head before turning toward me.

"It's time for you to go," Kington said.

"Where am I going? Back to Brentson? Back to the apartment that I was staying in?" I wanted to ask if I had a say in any of this, but I refrained for now because I wanted to see what he would say.

"Back to the apartment."

"I don't want to go back there. Brentson is where my home is, and I should be able to stay there. After all, you said I would be safer once we announced that I was a member of the Cross family so why does it feel like I'm still being kept in hiding?"

I sounded like a brat in my mind because the apartment that I'd been staying in was stunning. I had everything I needed outside of the people who'd welcomed me with open arms, and I'd had enough of hiding or living in fear.

Kingston didn't say anything, and I glanced at Nash. I was slightly unsure about where I was going with this, but I knew it had to be said, so I continued.

"If you've been watching my roommates without issue and keeping them safe without them being aware, what else would need to be done to make sure that I can live on campus and still have a somewhat normal college experience, at least for the time being?"

I could see that Kingston was thinking about my suggestion which was better than a flat out "this won't work."

"I also think you'll understand if I don't want to let Raven out of my sight. Not after I thought I'd lost her. Twice."

Both Kingston and I swung around to look at Nash. I hadn't been expecting him to say anything and it was clear Kingston hadn't either.

Kingston's gaze narrowed at Nash. "Anything that deals with figuring out Raven's security measures is between me and Raven."

"The hell it is. You've only known her for a short period of time, whereas I've known her for years. I love her."

A small jolt of electricity ran through my body because of his words.

Kingston didn't seem as taken aback by Nash's declaration as I thought he might be. "You know I didn't have to let you into her room at all."

"And I thank you for doing so, but it doesn't change any of the feelings I have about you making me think she'd died and then allowing one of your henchmen to knock me out."

Kingston smirked. "Landon didn't mention that part."

Nash acted as if he was going to advance on Kingston and I put my hand up on his chest to stop him. "Can both of you stop it? We are all adults and can talk without taunting one another."

I could feel Nash's heart racing against my hand, and I knew he wanted to do anything but take my advice. But to have them fighting in this hotel room would do nothing to further the goal here and that was to find out who was trying to kidnap me.

"First, don't talk about me as if I'm not standing right here with the both of you. Can we focus on finding out who wants to kidnap me? And why?"

That seemed to deflate Nash's anger and wiped the look from Kingston's face. How they'd decided that egging each other on was more important than focusing on protecting my life was beyond me.

"What have you found that made you realize that I wasn't involved, and how might that lead to us finding who is actually behind this?"

Kingston stared Nash down before glancing at me. "It's obvious that whoever is doing this has the means to hire someone to pull this whole plan off, even if the person who was hired was incompetent."

I thought about what Kingston said and chose my words carefully. "So someone with money... that could be anyone. Who's to say the person didn't take out a loan in order to be able to hire someone to kidnap me?"

"That's a bit far-fetched, but if someone is desperate enough, I wouldn't put it past them."

My legs began to move as I tried to process everything that was being said. "Until we know, I want a firm commitment that you two won't treat me like a child and that I can go back to having some semblance of a life once I leave this hotel room. Got it?"

Both men in front of me seemed surprised by my outburst. Although they both thought they had my best interests at heart, I was always going to be my own best advocate.

"We'll look into it. For now, you should go back to the apartment in NYC until we can double-check things at the place in Brentson. We can make sure that Nash gets back to wherever he was staying."

"What part of I'm staying with her—"

I cleared my throat loudly. "Can we not do this again? It's not productive."

"I'm coming with her." Nash had to get the last word.

Kingston let out a deep breath. He was clearly over our shit.

"Fine."

23

RAVEN

I ran a finger across my phone and watched as my screen lit up. I finally had time to check my phone after all of the excitement of the day because we were on our way out of New York City.

I found my texting app and was surprised that I didn't have any text messages. Izzy would have been worried, so something was up.

"Kingston, why don't I have any text messages?" He'd told me that Izzy, Lila, and Erika were safe, and I had nothing to worry about when it came to them because his team was watching over him. There were only two reasons why Izzy wouldn't have been texting me. One was if she thought I was fine, but even then, she'd still check in. The other was because she didn't have access to her phone which would potentially lead me to think that she might be hurt or dead.

Kingston looked back at me through the rearview mirror before focusing on the road ahead again. "We've been answering them on your behalf. It was a way to keep suspicion down while also not letting anyone know where you were."

I sat back in my seat and raised an eyebrow. Our eyes once again met in the rearview mirror. "But the whole point was for people to think I was dead to temporarily stop anyone from coming after me. If the person after me had seen the text messages, they would have known that either I was alive or someone had my phone. They would have probably assumed the former."

"If they had, they would have been lured to one of my properties and would have easily been taken out. And I have to disagree with you about one thing. They would have more than likely thought someone had stolen the phone or something, seeing as how the car explosion caused enough of a spectacle that they would lean toward someone having stolen the phone versus you still being alive. At least until the announcement at the gala was made."

The statement and the finality in his voice made me quiet. He made a couple of great points and had way more experience than me when it came to keeping people safe, so what more was there to argue about?

I wasn't fond of what he or a member of his team had done, lying to Izzy, but I could see why he'd done it.

I read through what Kingston's team had told Izzy before I began to compose a message to Izzy.

Me: *I'm on my way back to Brentson now. Can't wait to see you!*

When she didn't answer my text right away, I turned to look out of the window closest to me. Watching the scenery fly by as we drove back to Brentson was therapeutic in a way.

It was another homecoming of sorts, and this felt much different than my drive back to town just a few weeks ago.

First, I had Nash by my side. The last time we'd attempted to enter an SUV, we'd gotten split apart and the one carrying me exploded. This time, we were seated side by side and Nash was cradling my hand in his lap. It also felt as if he was doing it because he was worried the moment he let go, I'd disappear.

Second, my emotions about my return to Brentson were much different this time around. I felt much more at ease about my return and was ready to get back to some semblance of the life that I'd had before I'd gone into hiding for several days. I'd settled into a life on campus that included a fairly normal routine as a college student and all of that had gotten tossed to the side when danger appeared once again. But now, I was determined to reclaim my life in any way that I could until whoever wanted to harm me ceased to exist.

I knew that killing them would be the only outcome of this. I had complete confidence that Nash or Kingston wouldn't stop until whoever organized this was dead.

A few weeks ago, I probably would have been upset by such a result. But now, it was what they deserved.

"What's wrong?" Nash's question broke through my concentration on the matter at hand.

"Nothing. Why?"

"You clenched your hand around mine. What were you thinking about?"

It looked like I couldn't hide my thoughts any longer. "I was just thinking about how much my mindset has changed about certain things."

Confusion briefly clouded Nash's face. "You mean like manifesting?"

I shrugged. "I was thinking more along the lines of killing the asshole who is causing all of this. I was so scared when I watched you kill Paul, but now I kind of don't give a fuck."

So many emotions crossed Nash's face that it almost looked comical. He looked stunned to hear that come out of my mouth.

When he didn't say anything, I chuckled. "You okay? Wasn't expecting me to say that, huh?"

"Nope. Not even a little bit."

My laughter grew and I watched as Nash's lips twitched. "I don't know. It feels like an eye for an eye type of situation and normally, I'm not like that, but I feel differently about all of this. I'm over it and if that means murdering someone who tried to harm me, then so be it. I want to have a life again."

"And I want to be involved in your life, no matter what." Nash picked up my hand and brought it to his lips.

I shook my head with a smile on my face. He was laying it on thick, but I wouldn't lie and say that I didn't enjoy it. I pulled my hand back when he lowered it and tried my best to rest my head on his shoulder. It was more difficult due to my seat belt, but I managed.

"I have so much to make up for." He mumbled the words, so I wasn't sure if he wanted me to hear them or not.

I enjoyed the sentiment, nonetheless. The nerves that I had about returning were still there, but with Nash by my side, I felt safe and secure, something that had always been in flux since my mother passed away.

The rest of the ride back to Brentson was uneventful and I stepped out of the SUV, book bag in hand, and closed my eyes as the crisp air greeted me. The rush I felt as the cool air touched my skin felt amazing. It made me feel more alive than I had the last time I'd been standing in this same place. Instead of feeling dread at having to get into an SUV and being whisked to places unknown, I felt happy because I was at home once more. I glanced around to see if anything out of the ordinary was around, but I didn't notice anything.

Nash walked around the back of the SUV and grabbed my book bag from me. I nodded at Nash before I turned to Kingston, who had let me out of the vehicle and said, "I guess this is goodbye for now."

He nodded and then said, "It is, but we'll be in touch. And know that there is always someone here watching you, especially until we catch the fucker who tried to kidnap you."

There was an awkward moment where I wasn't sure whether I should hold my hand out, give him a hug, or thank him. When he stuck out his hand, I was relieved because the awkwardness evaporated.

I shook his hand and gave him a small smile. "Thanks for everything and I'm sure I'll see you soon."

Kingston hesitated for a moment and turned to shake Nash's hand too. I noticed that he squeezed Nash's hand harder than necessary, and I rolled my eyes. He was taking this older brother thing a little too far.

"Okay, enough," I said as I took a step back. "We need to get inside, and you need to leave before anyone notices you."

Together, Nash and I walked away from the SUV and up to the front porch of my home on campus. When we turned around, we saw the SUV we'd been traveling in pull away from the curb and take off down the street.

"Can you turn around so I can dig into my backpack?"

Nash did as I asked, and I fished around for my keys. Once I had them in hand, I opened the front door and both Nash and I stepped inside the house. I was happy to see that nothing had changed since I'd been gone. Not that it should have because I hadn't been gone that long, but I would be lying if I said that I hadn't thought that things might have been shifted around, much like I'd felt when I returned to Brentson for the first time in two years.

I found Izzy on the couch on her computer. She looked up when she saw me in the hallway. "Hey! There you are! I just saw your text."

Izzy put her laptop on the cushion beside her and stood up. She then came at me, almost at full speed, and I braced for impact. She threw her arms around me and gave me a huge hug. Once we broke apart, she stepped back and looked at Nash.

"Stop keeping her all to yourself. She needs to go to class and hang out with us too."

It took me a moment to understand what was going on. The person who sent Izzy the text messages must have made something up about Nash taking me somewhere as an excuse to explain why I wasn't here or answering my text messages or phone calls regularly.

Nash tucked me into his side and said, "I'm making up for lost time."

Izzy smiled at both of us. "You know, since Raven returned, I wasn't a huge fan of you because of the asshole you'd become, but maybe I was wrong."

"And you and I both know how hard it was for you to admit that," I said teasingly.

It was Izzy's turn to roll her eyes at me. "You know why I

didn't care for him, so none of this is brand-new information to you."

She was right. I did know why she didn't like Nash and most of it had to do with me.

"I still don't like how you tried to manhandle her the night she was dancing with Landon at the frat party."

Nash's demeanor changed in the blink of an eye. He immediately became tense, and I knew it was because she mentioned Landon's name. "I won't apologize for anything I did that night."

I didn't know what Izzy had been expecting, but it was obvious she hadn't been expecting him to say that. Her eyes widened in surprise before she narrowed them.

I stepped away from Nash for a moment. "Okay, I'm over getting between people arguing about me today so can we settle this another time?"

"Fine. I'm just happy that you're back. Lila, Erika, and I missed you."

She gave me an even bigger hug this time and I squeezed her just as tightly as she squeezed me. "And I missed you all too."

24

NASH

"What's wrong?"

"Nothing is wrong, Nash."

I let her response hang in the air for a moment before I uttered another word. "I don't believe you."

Raven shifted, causing my arm to fall down to her waist before she said, "I'm sitting here, enjoying a quiet evening with you. What gave you the impression that something was wrong?"

I looked down at the top of Raven's head before looking back at the television in front of us. She lay on my chest while we were watching a television show that I don't think either one of us was really focusing on. Instead, it ended up being background noise that gave us something to listen to while we relaxed.

It was a few days after we'd both arrived back in Brentson, and we'd quickly fallen into a routine of alternating whose place we stayed at. Tonight we were at mine and spending quality time together where we were less likely to be disturbed. Not that I minded her roommates, but I also enjoyed having her to myself, although temporarily.

"Because you're being quiet. Something is on your mind, and I want to know what you're thinking about."

Raven sighed. "I'm thinking about us, alright?"

I knew something was up and I was happy that I'd pushed her on it. I'd been trying to be as understanding as I could possibly be and had been waiting for her to come to me with what was bothering her. But I'd had enough and decided that a different tactic might work in this scenario.

"What about us?"

"Are you even going to prepare?"

"Prepare for what?"

Raven moved so that she could sit up on her own and look straight at me. "For the Chevaliers stuff."

I didn't tell her exactly what my last task would entail because I wasn't sure. I'd guessed that it would be some sort of pop quiz to test our knowledge about the Chevaliers and its history. I was confident in what I knew about the society. It was now or never, and I was ready to just get this over with.

"If I haven't prepared by now, it's pointless. My final task is in a couple of hours."

"Okay..." Her voice trailed off as if she'd given up on questioning me.

"I've been preparing for years for this moment." Part of me wanted to keep this to myself, but the words just fell out of my mouth. She didn't know everything about the Chevaliers, but I was happy to share this with her. It was something that many people outside of the Chevaliers didn't know about. The time and effort that went into balancing trying to rise to a leadership position in the secret society, football, and my schoolwork was a lot. Although I couldn't tell her everything, I liked being able to at least admit that.

Raven nodded. "I thought so, but you seem to be pretty ambivalent about the whole thing."

"I realized that there were more important things to life. That's not to say that I don't want to succeed within the Chevaliers, but my priorities have shifted considerably."

"Nash, what are you talking about?"

My stare didn't waver from hers because she was what I was talking about. There were times over the course of the last few days where I could feel some of her hesitancy, including just a few moments ago. What I wanted her to know was that I was always going to be there for her, no matter what. When she left Brentson, she was still on my mind constantly. When I thought she was dead, I was determined to do anything in my power to avenge her death. Throughout it all, she remained in my mind.

And in my heart.

"Being with you has always been the real deal for me. I would go to the ends of the earth to make sure that you're happy. And anyone who causes you to feel any pain or shame will have to deal with all of the hell that I would bring their way. I won't stop at anything to make sure that you feel nothing but secure in every aspect of your life."

"It's not your job to—"

I turned my body completely toward her and fought the urge to slam my fist on the table. Instead, I took a deep breath to calm myself because it was obvious to me that she didn't understand. And I knew I deserved a fair share of the blame, especially for how I treated her when she first came back to Brentson. "The hell it isn't. You've had to deal with tragedy after tragedy all by yourself. You deserve to have someone who can shoulder some of the stress you have, and I promise to take that on. Even when I thought I hated you, I would have done anything for you. It's why staying away from you was out of the question even when it made the most sense."

Her mouth opened and then closed. When she did it again, I confirmed with myself that I'd shocked her into silence, and I couldn't hide my smirk any longer. She didn't have a response and I enjoyed the thrill that I got from it.

My hand grazed her cheek, and I enjoyed the feel of my skin on hers. I turned my hand over so that I could cup her cheek and she leaned into my touch. I gave her a tender kiss on the lips that ended with both of us smiling.

She settled back against my chest and asked, "Do you think Landon will be there?"

Her question almost ruined the good mood I was in. Almost.

I was proud of myself for controlling the urge to growl. "He might be, but it doesn't matter if he's there or not. The outcome will still be the same."

"You're going to beat him?"

"Without a fucking doubt."

My self-assurance made Raven chuckle, but I was serious. He didn't stand a chance against me, but given his status as a member of Cross Sentinel, part of me wondered if he would be there tonight. Did it make any sense for him to be there? What was the point of him doing any of this to begin with?

It brought me back to how much I really knew about Landon Brennan, and I realized it wasn't that much. Then again, it wasn't as if any of that mattered when it came down to it. All that mattered was completing this next objective.

My phone vibrated on the coffee table, and I reached to grab it. I found a text message waiting for me and as I read it, my eyes narrowed.

Tomas: *There's been a change in venue for tonight's task. You're to come to the following address.*

The address that was listed in the next text message didn't make any sense.

"What's wrong?"

My change of expression must have alerted Raven.

"There's been a change of venue for tonight's task. Thought it was going to be at the Chevalier Manor, but now it's some address I don't recognize off the top of my head."

"Look it up to see if we recognize anything around it?"

I was already a step ahead of her as I clicked the address and watched as my map app showed me the location. There looked to be nothing there, but much like the cabin I owned, there could be a residence there that hadn't been put on the map. It was potentially remote enough for that to be the case. I showed Raven my phone so that she could see where it was on the map, and she shook her head.

"I don't know where that is."

I figured the chance of her knowing this location was low. I moved the map around before I said, "It might be someplace near the road we take when we drive to the cabin, but other than that, I'm not sure. I've never driven that way."

"I don't like this," muttered Raven. "Something about this doesn't seem right."

I didn't bother trying to reassure her about it because I felt the same way. "What would make you feel better about it?"

"If I had some way to contact you to make sure that you were okay."

I thought about it for a moment. "How about I text you when I get there and let you know that everything looks okay?"

Raven nodded slowly as if she didn't really trust what I was saying, but she didn't voice any opposition to my plan.

While I didn't voice it to Raven, this change of plans had me puzzled. Was the change in venue supposed to throw everyone off?

Too bad, it wouldn't work, at least when it came to me. I was determined for the Chevalier trials to end tonight and for me to be on top. I looked down at my phone again and saw that I had forty-five minutes before I needed to be at the new location.

It was time.

25

NASH

The moon guided me as I cruised along the deserted road. My destination wasn't exactly clear, but at least there was more light than I thought there would be. The closer I drove to the address that had been sent to me, the more I felt as if something was wrong. But I checked and then I double-checked the address and that was the one that Tomas had provided me in the text message he sent.

Still, I was confused about this taking place in the middle of nowhere, but it wasn't the weirdest thing I'd done as a Chevalier. Not by a long shot.

It took a few more minutes, but soon I was pulling my sports car to a stop in front of a cabin that was reminiscent of the one that grandfather owned before Bianca and I inherited it. I picked up my phone and noticed that my phone jumped between having one bar of service and none. It wasn't surprising given where I was, but I also wondered if this was done on purpose.

What was also strange about this was I didn't see any

other cars around. Usually there was at least some activity, but this felt different. It was strange, but I was as prepared as I was ever going to be. The only thing I was kicking myself about was not bringing a gun because everything about this raised red flags for me.

But if this was supposed to be the last task, then so be it.

When I turned off the car, I thought I would be surrounded by darkness, but the moon helped tremendously. It was exceptionally bright to the point where it provided a glow that gave me the ability to see without having to use the flashlight on my phone. I flipped over to my messaging app and typed a quick text to Raven.

Me: *Made it but am not sure about any of this. I don't think anyone is here, but I'll text you in a few minutes to confirm.*

I wouldn't be able to text her while I was doing the task, but I would make time to do so before anything got started. The great debate about whether my phone would send the message began.

When I stepped out of the car, I made sure to scan the periphery of the house. From what I could see, it was deserted, just as I'd suspected. Seeing as how no one was here to greet me, nor were the other candidates for Chevalier chairmanship here, I got the feeling that I was walking into a trap, but I refused to turn back.

Someone obviously wanted to get me alone and now they had the opportunity. If this meant bringing all of this shit to an end, so be it.

Instead of walking straight toward the house, I tread slowly into the woods in hopes of somewhat concealing myself. I regretted driving up to the cabin as opposed to parking farther away to hide that I was in the area. Whoever wanted me to come here would see my car, but I hoped they wouldn't know where I was. I tried to remain as quiet as possible in order to see or hear if someone was near me. Instead of walking up to the front porch, I figured the best approach might be to go around the back.

I walked around the periphery of the house, but nothing looked out of the ordinary other than the property being abandoned. It was obvious that the area was well kept in spite of no one being here, so I wouldn't have been surprised if the Chevaliers did own this property, but I still couldn't shake the feeling that something was wrong.

When I reached the back of the house, I saw that there was a small light on in the back of the house. Either someone left it on and then left, or someone else was here.

I paused to see if I could hear anything in the distance but heard nothing. The hairs on the back of my neck stood up. I knew that I was being watched.

I adjusted my body in preparation for something to come out and attack me. I looked down and noticed that from what I could see, there weren't any wires that I could trip over to alert anyone that I was there.

"Hello, Henson."

I didn't try to take the time to think about whether I recognized who spoke or not. I swung around, prepared to fight whoever was behind me, but nothing happened.

Instead, I found Tomas standing there with a gun pointed at me. I hadn't been expecting the person to be holding a gun.

I stared at him for a moment, hoping that this might have been one sick joke, but nothing on his face indicated that this was a game. I slowly raised my hands, showing that I didn't have anything in them and asked, "There isn't a Chevalier chairmanship task tonight, is there?"

"I'm sorry to report that there isn't. Hand over your phone."

I debated arguing with him about it, but the gun in my face gave me pause. It wouldn't be the smartest thing I'd ever done. But hell, was coming to this place when I suspected something was up smart?

Handing over my phone to Tomas was probably the worst thing I could do at this moment. I remembered that I didn't text Raven back like I said I would. Deep down, I hoped that alerted her that something was amiss, but I also didn't know if she got my first message either.

Fuck.

I couldn't dwell on that, however. My focus needed to be on Tomas and getting his gun away from him. I decided to try my best to distract him from worrying about my phone.

"I don't know why you're doing this, but it doesn't need to happen. You don't need to throw your whole life away because of this."

"That's funny, because this is the one thing that would make me feel more alive than anything I've ever done in my entire life, including becoming a Chevalier. Turn around and go into the cabin."

"I'll forget that all of this is happening if you just let me go back to my car and drive away."

"Shut the fuck up and go up the stairs."

For now, it seemed as if he'd forgotten that he'd asked for my phone. I hoped that no one would try to text or call me because he might hear the phone vibrating and then remember what he'd asked for.

I briefly looked behind me before taking a step up the stairs and another. I refused to turn around completely if I could help it because I didn't want my back to him since he had a gun. The need to be aware of where he was at all times won out over the discomfort I had about walking backward.

Tomas followed me, standing a little too close for comfort, and when I reached the back door of the cabin, he walked around me to open the door. He shoved the door open and pointed the gun, gesturing for me to walk inside first. I did as he wanted because I didn't want to piss him off further.

When Tomas closed the door behind him, I took the opportunity to ask the question that had been on my mind since this all began. "Why are you doing all of this? What's the point?"

Tomas raised an eyebrow at me. "Are you really that fucking clueless?"

"I have no idea what you're talking about."

Tomas glared at me. I guess in an attempt to intimidate me into admitting that I knew more than I did, but I didn't react.

"Either you're the greatest actor of all time or you truly don't know."

I didn't know if him realizing that got me any brownie points, but I couldn't deny that I was happy that the guy who had the gun had calmed down, however slightly.

"I don't know what you're alluding to, Tomas." I hoped my words would further reassure him that I wasn't the enemy, even though he clearly thought I was.

"Your father."

I didn't know what I'd been expecting him to say, but that hadn't been it. I'd thought the reason why he was holding me at gunpoint was because of something I did. "What did he do?"

"Killed my older sister."

There was nothing I could do to stop my mouth from dropping open at that news. My father was scum, but I was surprised to hear that he had anything to do with the death of another Chevalier's family member. I had assumed that, like me, he had killed someone in order to become a Chevalier, but this was different.

"Killed your sister? He did what?"

Tomas nodded furiously. "He murdered her and now I want him to experience the same type of hurt that I feel every single fucking day."

I tried to keep my face impassive while my heart was racing. His confession had thrown a wrench into my plan to get out of here, but maintaining a cool head and getting out alive were still the most important things I needed to do.

I took a deep breath to calm my racing heart and asked, "What happened?"

Tomas cut his eyes over to me before looking back at the fire. "My sister was one of the women that your father called on through his connection to Kiki Hastings. It's not something I wanted her to do, but she was determined and there was nothing I could do to stop her."

I nodded, trying to empathize with him but also looking for an opportunity to overtake him and knock the gun he was holding out of his hand.

"But how did he kill her?"

"He didn't actually pull the trigger, but he was the last one to see her alive."

I tilted my head to the side as I repeated what he said in my brain. "How do you know he was the last one to see her?"

"Kiki told me just before she was killed. I've been planning this ever since."

I'd known some things about Kiki Hastings, but not a lot. I vaguely remembered hearing about Kiki's death, and it hadn't been that long ago but, to be honest, I didn't know her well enough to feel strongly about it one way or the other.

"And because of this, you decided to avenge your sister's death by coming after me?"

"Yes. Do you know who else was involved with Kiki? Your bitch."

"Don't you dare refer to her as such." I know it wasn't wise to piss him off, but I didn't care. I refused to hear any slander when it came to Raven and if he wanted to kill me over it, so be it.

Tomas's smile made my skin crawl and I wanted to tackle him, but I knew better. I needed to keep him talking so that he admitted everything and I would have all of the answers I wanted.

"What does Raven have to do with any of this?"

Tomas leaned up against the fireplace and said, "It was a coincidence that she was brought back here when she was. I had nothing to do with that, but I was thankful, nonetheless, especially when I did my research about how much she'd hurt you. It was easy to see that you were still hung up on her and I wanted to hurt your father like he'd hurt me. So my plan was to kidnap and kill Raven, which would make you do your damnedest to hunt down whoever murdered her, and then I would kill you and deliver your body to your father personally because, at that point, I would have felt vindicated and truly not have a care in the world anymore because my mission was done. But Paul fucked up and got caught, so I had to readjust."

"So you hired Paul, the guy who tried to kidnap Raven?"

Tomas nodded. "I had to trick you when I came and saw your handiwork and acted as if I was seeing Paul for the first time. When you discovered him, he became a liability that I couldn't risk. I should be thanking you for taking care of that."

"You're welcome," I said sarcastically. "What I don't understand is why didn't you just go after my father instead of coming after me?"

"You aren't so bright now, are you?"

I glanced down at the gun before choosing to focus all of my attention on Tomas. "I guess not."

Tomas raised his hand like he might hit me with the gun, and I was prepared to grab it out of his hand if he attempted to slam it down on my head. But he didn't.

He quickly gained control of his emotions and lowered his hands. It was almost as if a light switch had been turned on and he was once again back to his calm and cool demeanor.

"I wanted you both to suffer. Your suffering would hurt him and then when I finally killed you, it would be like he's on the edge of dying, but he was still alive, having to live through the trauma of losing his son every single day. And I would have enjoyed every minute of it."

When there was a flash of light out of the window, it drew Tomas's attention temporarily away from me and toward the source. I knew that this was my opportunity to react, and I did. Without fully formulating a plan, I tackled him to the ground and the gun went flying out of his hand.

I landed a punch to his nose and heard him howl in pain. When I was preparing to strike him again, he headbutted me. The pain radiated through my skull and knocked me off of him.

In the time it took me to recover, Tomas gained the upper hand and slammed his fist into my stomach, forcing me to double over in pain. It took me a second to recover before we began trading blows. Fighting him proved to be hard because we had similar training. It wasn't going to be easy to overcome him, but I was more than willing to rise to the challenge.

Tomas threw me off of him and then sat up. While I was trying to catch my breath, I watched as he looked around the room. He was probably trying to find his gun and I knew there was no way I could let him get it. If he did, I knew that he would have no issue pulling the trigger.

I scrambled to get up and saw him attempting to do the same. I pushed myself and happened to get up first. Adrenaline careened through my body as I sprinted over to him and grabbed him by his hair. I yanked him back as hard as I could and before he could react, I threw another punch to his face. He howled in agony, and I couldn't deny that I loved the sound of it.

I let his head go and walked around him, hearing it slam against the ground, but I didn't bother to look back. The groans that came from his lips told me that he was still alive, which was what I wanted. I grabbed the gun and put the safety on before taking the bullets out.

"Guns aren't really my style," I said as I placed the gun on the mantel. I ran a hand across my lip and found blood on the back of my hand. He would pay for that too.

I looked to my left and found something I hadn't been expecting, but that made me happy, nonetheless. A small smile appeared on my face as the thoughts of what I could do to him flashed through my mind. I bent down to pick it up as Tomas groaned again.

"You know, I told you that I would have forgotten this entire thing if you would have just let me go. But now I'm feeling... vindictive."

I turned around and showed him what I held in my hands. Tomas's eyes widened and I couldn't hide my grin. I slapped the handle into the palm of my hand.

"Look, I didn't mean for any of this to happen..."

I snorted. "No, you didn't think that you would be in the position where I would be in control. Hiding behind that gun did a number on you. You should have stuck to our training or killed me out front when you had the chance. Arrogance is one hell of a drug, isn't it?"

Tomas held his hand up, in much the same position I had when he'd approached me with the gun. "None of this is necessary, Nash."

"Oh now it's Nash instead of Henson. That's adorable."

I raised the axe and swung, hitting him in the leg. If I thought that he'd screamed loud before, it was no match for the scream he'd just let out. I smirked as I swung again, hitting him in the other leg. The thrill that shot through me was similar to what I felt on the football field whenever I threw the ball and one of the guys would end up in the end zone for a touchdown.

Seeing him in pain was exhilarating as I swung again. All

the shit he'd caused Raven and me because he had it out for my father was inexcusable, even though I knew my father was a piece of shit. If he wanted to go after anyone, it should have been my father and my father alone.

"Nash!"

I stopped midswing and looked over my shoulder.

I looked up and saw who was behind me, but all I could do was nod. I couldn't catch my breath quick enough to greet Raven and Kingston when I saw that they were standing there. Raven rushed over to me, her eyes and hands running over every inch of my skin to make sure that I was okay.

"We'll deal with him now."

But she and Kingston weren't alone. They were joined by Parker Townsend, not only the leader of the New York City chapter of the Chevaliers but probably one of the most important Chevaliers currently. Much of what the Chevaliers decided to do and their goals were suggested by the New York City chapter and it was only a matter of time before he ended up running the entire organization. I didn't expect to see him here tonight.

"How long were you guys standing there?"

"Long enough," Kingston answered for everyone.

My eyes moved from Kingston to Parker and finally to Raven. "You all could have stopped me from trying to kill him."

"But we didn't," Parker said. "We let it continue because this was justice served."

"He blames my father for his sister's death."

"Tomas's sister was going through a lot and had a bunch of demons that she was battling. As far as we know, she knew your father because of his tendencies to look for company through Kiki Hastings."

Raven jerked when Parker said her name, confirming for me that it was the woman that she'd met with when she was debating about becoming an escort.

"It would be hard to say that your father was the reason she killed herself, even if he was the last one she saw."

"You knew about the circumstances surrounding her death?"

Parker nodded. "I did. What I didn't know was that Tomas was planning all of this, but he'll have to answer for it now that you held back and didn't kill him."

I wanted to murder him and watch as the life left his body, but that would be the easy way out for him. He deserved to suffer for the rest of his fucking life and if beating and torturing him to within an inch of his life would lead to it, then so be it.

"Nash?"

I looked toward Parker before tucking Raven into my side. She had her arms wrapped around my body, trying her best to support me in any way she could.

"Congratulations on becoming the next chairman of the Brentson University Chapter of the Chevaliers."

The air left my lungs at his declaration. With everything going on, it had been the last thing I was expecting.

"But how?"

Parker took a step toward me. "It was clear pretty early on that it was you who was meant for this job, and it was what I'd expected all along, which was why I'd lured Raven back here. It was a test to see how you would react and I'm proud of what you've done even if it wasn't the most... orthodox."

I glanced at Tomas, who was still withering on the floor in pain, before looking back at Parker. "Well, I guess all I can say is thank you."

"You don't sound too thrilled about it."

"It was unexpected, and I went into this 'challenge' not caring as much once I thought I might have an opportunity to catch who was trying to hurt Raven. That was the only thing that mattered to me."

"I'll ignore the fact that you just told one of your superiors that you didn't care about the organization you are a part of."

My eyes widened in surprise. "No, I'm happy that I have this opportunity to—"

"Don't worry about it. I understand the position that you're in and why you would feel this way. None of this will take away from you having the chairmanship unless you choose not to accept."

I looked down at Raven and she gave me a wide grin. I then looked back at Chairman Townsend and said, "I accept."

"Good. Now there should be some people here any minute to collect Tomas and clean this mess up. After all, it's Chevalier property." He glanced at Tomas, who was still withering on the ground. "He'll have to answer for more than just the things he plotted against you."

When he and Kingston turned to walk away, a thought popped into my head. "Chairman Townsend?"

He turned to look back at me and Kingston did the same.

"Were you sending text messages from an unknown number to me?"

Parker briefly looked confused. "No. Why would I? I have more important things to do."

"Doesn't mean you couldn't hire someone to do it."

"Nash." The way Kingston said my name had a slight warning to it. It seemed as if, this time, I was walking on a thin line, but I didn't care.

But Kingston had no authority over me. Yes, he was a powerful Chevalier, but I was the chairman now and the number of fucks that I had right now was zilch. I'd just fought for my life and won. Now I wanted answers.

"I'm just trying to find out the truth. I received a few text messages, and I don't know who the hell is sending them."

As if the sender somehow knew that I was speaking about the messages, my phone vibrated.

Unknown Number: *Nothing about tonight is what you think it is. Tread carefully.*

A whole lot of good that text message did now, but it did leave another unanswered question. Who the hell was sending these text messages?

26

RAVEN

I closed my textbook with a resounding thud and stretched my arms above my head. I was over studying, and it was time for me to head back home.

A quick glance at my phone proved that it was late and that the library would be closing soon. I suspected that not many people were left here and that I should get home soon.

I packed all of my things up. All that was left were a couple of books that I needed to bring up to the front desk because I wasn't checking them out. I stood up and stretched, letting my body feel the joy of not having to sit down any longer.

I picked up my phone again to see if I'd received a text from Nash. It had been a while since I'd heard from him. When I found nothing from him, I put the phone in my bag with a sigh. I couldn't help but feel dejected.

He'd been busy with a Chevalier meeting tonight as the new incoming chairman and I hadn't heard from him in a couple of hours. With Tomas now being held who knows where, I'd felt more safe, but I also found myself spending less time with my boyfriend and that sucked. I would be happier when the college football season wound down because he'd be less busy with that, and his schedule would free up considerably.

I smoothed down the black skirt I decided to wear today and reached for the books. But I never touched them.

Something grabbed me around the waist and covered my mouth before I could scream. The person pulled me away from the desk I was studying at and into a row full of books. I quickly lost sight of the desk and my bag as I tried to fight against the hold the person had on me.

The assailant leaned down in my ear and said, "Hi, Little Bird."

I visibly relaxed when I recognized the voice. Part of me wanted to turn around and shove him for scaring me so badly, but I also couldn't lie and say I wasn't turned on by what he'd just done.

"If I remove my hand, you promise not to scream?"

I nodded my head quickly and he slowly loosened his grip on my mouth but didn't give me an inch when it came to the arm wrapped around my waist. He nibbled on my ear, and I shivered.

"We shouldn't be doing this in here."

"When has that ever stopped us? Did you wear this for me?" Nash's voice was low as the hand that had been holding my mouth made its way to my skirt. He ran his fingers along the tights I had on before making his way back to the skirt.

"I didn't, because I didn't know if I was going to see you tonight," I said, barely above a whisper.

Although I suspected that the library was mostly empty, I didn't want us to get caught either. The likelihood of that happening would significantly increase the closer we got to closing time because the students who worked the late shift would be coming around to make sure the library was empty before closing everything up.

"Well then, I don't feel nearly as bad for what I'm about to do."

Nash loosened the hold he had around my waist and turned me so that I was face-first against the bookshelf. With both of his hands now available, he had free rein to explore every inch of me and he acted as if he had no time to waste.

His hands immediately went back to the skirt and flipped it up. My ass would have been exposed if it wasn't for the tights I'd decided to wear to protect my skin from the cooler weather that had descended upon Brentson. He gripped, massaged, and slapped my ass, causing me to grow wetter by the second. Nash knew exactly what he was doing and had me right where he wanted me.

I felt it before I heard it. The sound of my tights ripping filled the air and I covered my own mouth to hide my shock. I'd had an inkling that he might try something like this when he turned me around, but I had no idea he would act on it.

I should have known better than to underestimate him.

I briefly thought back to him taking me out to the balcony and us fucking just above the party that his parents threw at their mansion. He'd threatened me with ripping my dress then and now he'd torn into something entirely different.

His hand moved to turn my face to the side so that he could lay a hard kiss on my lips. When we broke apart, his blue eyes reached mine and I swallowed hard as I tried to prepare myself for what was next.

He laid another rough kiss on my lips as his fingers

decided that the best course of action was to play in the hole he'd just created. Would he be buying me another pair of tights after this was all over? Yes, but right now, I couldn't give a shit less about the state of my clothes.

As we kissed, he ran a finger from my pussy to my ass and back again. I leaned into his touch while we kissed, hoping that he would get the hint and move my panties to the side so that he could fuck me properly.

He continued to tease me until I broke the kiss. I couldn't take it anymore and I wanted him now.

"If you don't fuck me, I'll—"

"You'll do what, Little Bird? When will you get that I'm the one that's in control of your pleasure?"

He growled when I grinded against his hand. I didn't care who was in control of what as long as it all eventually led to him fucking me.

Pleasure soared within me as he finally shifted my panties, and I felt his fingers get dangerously close to where I needed him most.

"I can feel how wet you are from here." He mumbled several curse words before finally giving me what I was desperate for. He buried a finger inside of me and I almost cried in relief.

Any thoughts I had of being a smart-ass or arguing with him about his need to tease me fled my mind. All I could think about was my impending orgasm and how quickly I knew he was going to get me there. My grip on the bookshelf tightened as I moaned quietly while he fucked me with his fingers until he suddenly stopped moving.

"You're going to have to be quiet, baby. Got it?"

I nodded. It was as if he was warning me about what was

to come, and there was nothing I could do but strap in and prepare for the ride of my life.

And that was when it began.

Nash held on to my waist with one hand while he used the other to drive me into another dimension.

"Fuck. You don't know how long I've been waiting for this. All I could think about was this sweet pussy when I should have been focusing on learning my new duties."

I could feel my orgasm building and it was as if he knew what was coming too because he stopped and removed his hand from me completely.

Before I could turn around and snap at him in protest, I heard some shuffling and soon felt the head of his cock on my ass.

"Did you think I was going to leave you hanging?"

Before I could answer his question, he pushed down on my back slightly, forcing my ass to stick out more. When his cock was stationed at my entrance, I held my breath as I was ready to embrace the feeling that I knew was about to flow over me. When he slid into me, it took everything in me not to scream.

Feeling him glide in and out of me made me feel as if I was walking through paradise. My orgasm was no match for him because soon my body felt as if I were careening out of control. I thought he might give me a moment to catch my breath once I'd gone over the edge.

But he didn't stop.

He fucked me through one orgasm and seemed to be determined to make sure that I at least had one more. His cock slammed into me with a hunger I didn't know existed.

My entire body was sensitive, and it didn't take long before another orgasm took my body over.

"I don't think I can do this again," I whispered.

"Yes, the hell you can," his words sounded more like grunts as he pounded into me.

I didn't want to admit that he was right, but then I felt my climax building once more. Nash never missed a beat as he reached around to the front of my body and found my clit.

"Take it, Little Bird. Take all of this."

That was all the encouragement I needed. I bit my lip as another orgasm took over me. Nash continued to glide his cock in and out of me until he, too, joined me.

"I love you," he said through the deep breaths he was attempting to take. He'd done his best to not lean against me. It was a miracle we hadn't taken the bookcase down with us.

Emotion leaped in my throat, although I barely heard him over the rush of the blood in my ears. "I love you too."

I looked over my shoulder at him once I finally caught my breath and said, "Same time next week? This time at Beyond the Page?"

Beyond the Page was a bookstore in town that had become a local hangout for many college students. I'd been to it a couple of times now. The vibe of the bookstore was relaxed, and it was a great place to get off campus temporarily.

Nash chuckled as he helped me fix my clothes. I laughed because I knew I looked hilarious, and I hadn't even gotten a glimpse of my hair yet.

"There's nothing we can do to fix this situation." I pointed down to my tights. "I'm going to get cleaned up and take these off because they are pointless now."

"I'll buy you a new pair." He paused as he admired his handiwork. "Why don't you hand me the keys to your car, and I'll drive around to the front so you don't have to walk too far in the cold? Then, when we get back to your place, I can make it up to you by taking everything as slow as you want it."

I couldn't help but smile at him as I leaned up on my tiptoes to give him a kiss.

"You have yourself a deal, Mr. Henson."

"Go, Nash! Go!"

I found myself cheering Nash on as the Bears took the field once more. They were playing Westwick University, one of Brentson University's rivals. This game ended up being a local match for both teams because the schools were maybe thirty minutes apart, allowing students and supporters from both schools to attend this matchup. Nash was playing fantastically, and I hoped that the Bears would get the win.

It felt good to be at a football game. It was the last one of the season, which was bittersweet for both Nash and me. The season coming to an end meant we would have more time together, but I also understood how much football meant to him.

It gave him a way to not only think smartly when it came to making great plays, but it was also a great outlet that helped him get his aggression out. And he had a lot of it.

Tomas was still being held somewhere and I wondered on

some days if Nash regretted not killing the man for what he'd done. The whole incident had been buried and kept from most of the Chevaliers on campus. Nash mentioned that some sort of leave of absence excuse was given for Tomas. The man that Tomas blamed for all of this, Van Henson, hadn't been made aware and his political career was still on track.

"Hey, Raven. Can I ask you something?"

Bianca's question brought me out of my thoughts. I glanced at her and gave her a smile. She and I decided that we would attend today's game together along with a friend of hers who we were still waiting to show up. I enjoyed having company while I watched the Bears kick ass.

"Sure. What's up?"

"Did you get the invite to the luncheon?"

"What luncheon?"

"The one that my sorority is hosting. I asked them to invite you and I noticed you weren't there, so I didn't know if you'd gotten left off of the guest list or what."

"I did get the invite, but with everything going on..."

Recognition appeared in Bianca's eyes. "It's fine and I completely understand. But I wanted you to know that we did want to extend an invitation to you in case you did want to come and see what we are all about. Just let me know. It would be a bit more informal than if it were our regular recruitment, but..."

I nodded and smiled. "I'll definitely let you know, Bianca. Thank you."

We both turned back to the game, and we watched as Nash threw a pass to Easton and Easton took off down the field.

"Part of me wants to root for him because I'll be rooting for the Bears, but it's also fucking *him*."

I turned my head slightly to look at Bianca, although I didn't want to take my eyes off the field. "You hate him that much, huh?"

"You don't even know."

"Does your brother know how much you dislike him?"

Bianca shrugged. "I don't think so. He probably thinks it's more along the lines of him treating me like a kid sister, but..."

I waited for her to continue, but when she didn't, I said, "Do you want to talk about it?"

"Nope." I saw Bianca shake her head twice out of the corner of my eye. "That's a story for another day and we should be focusing on the game."

"You know what?" Bianca said a few minutes later.

"What?"

"Being in the presence of anything related to Westwick University freaks me out."

"Why is that?" I'd heard of the university, given that it was so close to Brentson but had never been there. At least from what I could remember.

Bianca shrugged. "I think it's the vibe that the school gives off that has rubbed off on me the wrong way. I visited Iris there once and it almost felt like a dark cloud was over the school. I feel bad for Iris because she has to go there. She's the one who is supposed to be meeting us here."

I wondered where she was before I asked my question. "She can't transfer to Brentson?"

Bianca shook her head. "Nope. It's a family tradition for her to go to Westwick, so she's doing it."

Bianca didn't elaborate any more, and her short story made me feel guilty for someone I hadn't met. I pulled my coat tighter around my body, hoping to cover the fact that her words had caused me to shiver. The same vibes she was getting, I was feeling too, and I thought it had just been me.

"Bianca?"

Another voice dragged me away from my thoughts of what Westwick must be like and I turned to face the person who'd spoken. I came face-to-face with a brunette who'd dyed the ends of her hair purple. I stared at her for a moment to see if I recognized her, but nothing rang a bell.

"Iris, hey!" Bianca pulled her friend in for a hug.

I glanced back at the football game to keep an eye on what was going on. When I turned my head back toward them, I noticed that the two had finished hugging.

"Iris, this is Raven. She's my brother's girlfriend. Raven, this is my friend, Iris."

The two of us shook hands, and she said, "It's nice to meet you."

"Likewise," I said. "I'll move down and you can sit on the other side of Bianca."

As we readjusted, I happened to turn around and found something startling. My eyes scanned the crowd behind us and landed on a man who looked familiar, staring at us. It took me a second to piece together who it was and how I remembered him.

Soren Grant. The last time I'd seen him was at the Cross family gala. What was he doing at the game and on this side of the field?

It seemed as if his attention was drawn to Iris. He had to

know that I was watching him, right? Why didn't he stop staring at her?

Before I could say something, Bianca's phone rang and made me turn around to look at her. She took the phone out of her purse and rolled her eyes.

"What is it?" I asked.

"For the last couple of days, I've been getting these random text messages from an unknown number."

I raised an eyebrow just before I asked, "What did it say?"

"Warning me about something. When I texted back and asked for clarification, I didn't get a response. So I blocked the number, and they texted me from another number."

"Do you mind showing me what this text says?"

"I want to see too," said Iris.

Bianca shrugged her shoulders and showed the message to Iris before she handed the phone over so I could read the message.

Unknown Number: *Be careful what you wish for, B.*

My heart leaped into my throat because I could see what path this might be taking given what had happened to me once and to Nash multiple times. Nash and I never figured out who was behind those messages even after we'd mentioned them to Kingston and he had his team look into it.

I handed Bianca back her phone. "Are you wishing for something?"

"Not that I know of. It's so fucking strange," she replied.

"Maybe you should let Nash know." I made a note to myself to tell Kingston when I got the chance.

Bianca's face scrunched up for a moment. "It's nothing. I don't want to cause him to worry."

I turned back around to where I saw Soren last and noticed that he wasn't there anymore. I didn't mention any of what I'd just noticed to Bianca because there was a chance that I'd imagined the entire thing.

There was no way I wasn't telling Nash about the strange text messages Bianca was receiving, especially if this could have been related to what was going on with us. I didn't want to alarm her, but if these text messages were just getting started, there was no telling how far they would go or how much danger she could potentially be in if she were now on this person's radar.

I swallowed thoughts of what this could mean, and instead, I focused on the game that we had front-row seats at.

When the Bears won, I screamed in glee. It took some time for me to see Nash after the game, but when I did, I smiled at Iris and Bianca, who gave me small head nods.

Before I could make a move, Nash was jogging toward me and pulled me into his arms. When his lips landed on mine, I knew that this was where I was supposed to be.

Forever.

～

THANK you for reading Devious Heir! Although Nash and Raven's story is complete, you will see them in The Lies Beneath and Shattered Saint. Keep reading to find a sneak peek of them!

DON'T WANT to let Nash and Raven go just yet? Click HERE to grab a bonus scene featuring the couple!

. . .

WANT to join discussions about the Brentson University Series? Click HERE to join my Reader Group on Facebook.

PLEASE JOIN my newsletter to find out the latest about the Brentson University and my other books!

THE LIES BENEATH BLURB

Privilege has its secrets...

Westwick University is known for its prestige and pedigree for hundreds of years.

Many people would die to come here...

And some have come here and died.

There are lies buried within these walls that the world doesn't know about.

But I do.

It's what happens when your family has gone to the same college for generations.

Stories and secrets are passed down, making me yearn to know more.

I'm determined to discover if each and every one is true, but I'm distracted.

Because my new professor has taken a particular interest in me.

Or so I think.

I shouldn't be tempted because anything with him is forbidden.

But the way that he only has eyes for me has set me on edge.

I can't tell if there is something there or if I'm making it all up in my head.

Why would a billionaire, who is known for his solitary life after the death of his wife, want to teach here?

There's so much I don't know.

But I know that lies do nothing but lead to more lies.

And when I uncover the truth, the world will implode.

The Lies Beneath is the first book in a dark forbidden college romance duet that has enemies-to-lovers themes. This book may not be suitable for all readers due to dubious situations that might be triggering. It ends in a cliffhanger.

SNEAK PEEK OF THE LIES BENEATH
IRIS

The loud noises that were coming from the crowd fed into the energy I felt and that wasn't a good thing. This was supposed to be a minor reprieve from my daily routine and wasn't.

I hated being this nervous. This wasn't my scene but stepping outside of my comfort zone was supposed to be a good thing. Here I was at a football game watching my college's team play against our biggest rivals. I eagerly accepted Bianca's invitation to attend because I hadn't seen her in a while. But I didn't come here only to see her and to be mildly entertained for a few hours.

I wanted to get out of my dorm room and to socialize. The eeriness that surrounded Westwick University seemed to stay at the campus's gates and I was grateful. The secrets and darkness that were contained in centuries old architecture hadn't followed me to Brentson's football field. It felt as if a heavy boulder had been lifted off of my chest because I didn't have to worry about *him.*

Sports weren't my thing and me veering away from my

usual haunts should confuse him. Then again, if he was following me like I assumed he was, me changing my schedule slightly wouldn't mean a thing.

It would allow me time away from his gaze that sometimes rendered me useless. Whenever I was on campus, deep down I knew that he was always there, lurking in the shadows, watching every move I made.

As I shifted through the crowd, it was nice to be just one of many. It meant that I could blend in and not be the center of attention. Then again, the purple tips of my hair drew more attention than I'd been accustomed to, but I'd done that for my own benefit and no one else's. If people wanted to stare, then so be it.

Except for when it came to him.

The way he studied me was very measured and what it made me feel was almost indescribable. I was intimidated because I could never tell what he was thinking as he stared at me. It was as if he was undressing me with his eyes, slowly peeling back every layer of clothing until he had me bare.

But it was more than that. I noticed something in his measured approach. It seemed as if he enjoyed making me uncomfortable, but I could prove none of this. Simply staring at someone wasn't a cause for a concern, but it should be when it comes from him.

My professor.

And my boss.

How I ended up being a teaching assistant for him seemed to have happened by chance, but the more things happened, the more I wondered if it truly was a coincidence.

I forced myself to look into the crowd to see if I saw Bianca.

This was the first time in I didn't know how long that I didn't feel as if he was anywhere nearby.

And then it happened. My entire body felt as if it were on edge and that meant only one thing:

He was here.

I could feel his presence in this stadium full of people. That sounded strange, I know, but I also knew what this feeling was. I'd grown accustomed to him being in the same vicinity and the slight shift in air was there.

The coldness in his eyes sent a shiver down my spine even though I hadn't turned around to find out where he was today. No, I wouldn't give him the time of day.

Instead, I saw my friend's profile and walked straight to where she was sitting with another woman.

"Bianca?" I asked although I was pretty certain it was her. When she turned to face me, a wide grin took over her entire face.

"Iris, hey!" Bianca quickly pulled me into her arms before I had a chance to react. When we broke apart, she gestured to the woman standing beside her. "Iris, this is Raven. She's my brother's girlfriend. Raven, this is my friend, Iris."

"It's nice to meet you," I said as we shook hands.

"Likewise," Raven replied. "I'll move down and you can sit on the other side of Bianca."

I'd never heard Bianca mention Raven, but she seemed pretty adamant that we should meet and this was a perfect opportunity to do so.

I could feel him watching my every move as Bianca and Raven moved so that I could take the seat they were saving. As we got settled in our seats, I looked up and saw Raven look behind us and pause. That was when I knew she'd spotted him.

I hated that my instincts were right in this case. I debated saying something, but what was there to say? The professor that I was a teaching aide for was stalking me?

And I knew that he'd killed for me?

No. I couldn't say a word.

The ringing of Bianca's phone snatched our attention and I was relieved. It would save me from having to speak on something that could mean life or death.

The Lies Beneath is available for pre-order and will be released in 2023.

SHATTERED SAINT BLURB

This never should have happened…

He was supposed to be off limits.
    The one I couldn't have.
    There were lines that should never be crossed.
    At least until one fateful night
    That changed everything forever.
    Now we hated each other
    And nothing was going to change that.
    Ever.
    Or so I thought…

Shattered Saint is the first book in a dark college romance trilogy that has enemies-to-lovers themes. This book may not be suitable for all readers due to dubious situations that might be triggering. It ends in a cliffhanger and the next book in the series will be Shattered Sinner.

SNEAK PEEK OF SHATTERED SAINT

BIANCA

I wished I could make it stop.

The panic. The busyness that surrounded me.

All of it. I just wanted to make it all stop.

I took a swig from the glass of wine that I had in front of me and stared off into the nothingness that was my apartment. Sure, I'd had all I needed here and could do anything I wanted, but staring into the abyss seemed much more attractive to me.

On the surface, I had it all. I was the mayor's daughter who never wanted for anything monetarily. Sorority sisters who loved me. A mother and brother who cared for me. I would love to say that my father did too, but that was a story for a different day.

I took another big gulp of the wine in front of me. It was my third glass of the night. While I knew I should stop, I didn't want to. The alcohol was helping to numb the pain that I felt and I was alright with that for now.

Tomorrow I would deal with the consequences. After all

this was means for a celebration, even though it looked as if right now I was doing anything, but.

I'd kept my cool over the last couple of days and I was proud. I didn't have a sip of alcohol throughout my whole time in the city including at a gala I was forced to attend tonight. The urge to wash away my feelings about having to be somewhere I didn't want to be was strong, but I resisted.

But that ended as soon as I got back to my apartment. Once I was in the comfort of my own space, I took it as an opportunity to unwind, although by the looks of it, I probably should have stopped drinking a while ago.

I stared at the wine glass in front of me, debating with myself whether it made sense to drain the rest of the wine

I had to spend most of the night with my brother's best friend. The man I might have hated even more than my father.

Easton knew why I couldn't stand him ever since he did what he did to me. Yet, he did everything in his power to insert himself into my life just to piss me off. Although I would miss Nash, the sooner they both graduated from Brentson, the fucking better.

When my phone vibrated on the table, I was jolted out of the memories that I tried so hard to push away.

Unknown Number: *B, the fun has just begun.*

My mouth dropped open as I reread the text.

Who the hell was this?

Shattered Saint is available for pre-order and will be released in 2023.

ABOUT THE AUTHOR

Bri loves a good romance, especially ones that involve a hot anti-hero. That is why she likes to turn the dial up a notch with her own writing. Her Broken Cross series is her debut dark romance series.

She spends most of her time hanging out with her family, plotting her next novel, or reading books by other romance authors.

briblackwood.com

ALSO BY BRI BLACKWOOD

Broken Cross Series

Sinners Empire (Prequel)

Savage Empire

Scarred Empire

Steel Empire

Shadow Empire

Secret Empire

Stolen Empire

The Broken Cross Series Box Set: Books 1-3

The Ruthless Billionaire Trilogy

The Billionaire's Auction

The Billionaire's Possession

The Billionaire's Vengeance

Brentson University Series

Devious Game

Devious Secret

Devious Heir

The Westwick University Duet

The Lies Beneath

The Shattered Trilogy

Shattered Sinner

www.ingramcontent.com/pod-product-compliance
Lightning Source LLC
Chambersburg PA
CBHW050837190726
48286CB00007B/2119